Shyster & Shyster

Holy Taxation, Batman!

Misappear Series: Book 1

Francine Zane

Copyright 2016 by Francine Zane
Cover by C. Gallup
Edited by Marisha Huber

ISBN-13: 978-0692698723
ISBN 10: 0692698728

Shameless Rat Bastards
Publishing
shamelessratbastards.com

More from Francine Zane:

Misappear Series:

Fried Calamari (Short Story)

Lesbian Cure (September, 2016)

To Traci, Janet, Sarah and Brandee. Without you, I would not have had nearly as much fun.

Disclaimer: If you bought this book thinking it has anything to do with Batman, you are sadly mistaken. Please return this book for a full refund, with my apology. The mention of Batman is purely intentional suckup-age aimed at my children in the hope they may eventually read Shyster & Shyster and learn their mom really does have a sense of humor, warped though it might be.

ACKNOWLEDGEMENT

Thank you to Brycen for creating the word *misappear*. It really does best sum up how appearances are often deceiving. Thank you to Bailey and Colby for your first reads and to Ann and Marisha for your support and professional expertise. I applaud you all for adding to the success of this project.

Table of Contents

Prologue

My name is Lolla Brigida. No, not Gina Lollobrigida, the Italian actress from the sixties with perky breasts and a waist the size of a twelve-year-old. That Lollobrigida could turn the heads of everyone in the room just by walking in. The only things I share with Gina are the dark hair and the crappy knockoff of her name, thanks to a mother who was forever infatuated with Hollywood glamour. The only time people turn their heads my way is after I trip over my feet and land face first in the middle of the closest mud puddle. Sadly, that happens more often than I like to admit.

Maybe my own awkward history is why I agreed to buy into the established tax business without demanding a name change to something less sleazy than Shyster and

Shyster. Who am I to throw stones? The Shyster family can't control who they are any more than I had control over my mom naming me Lolla Brigida. Genetics did the rest.

I come from a long line of clumsy. My mother tripped and fell onto my father's penis and conceived me. She fell again when he ran out on her soon after finding out she was pregnant, meaning she tripped over her own two feet. He made a clean getaway. My grandmother tripped and fell onto the penis of a traveling salesman and conceived my mother. The salesman traveled right on down the road before she pulled her panties back up. My Uncle Huey tripped and fell into a wood chipper just six days after he recovered from a horrible bout of whooping cough that nearly cost him his life. He wasn't so lucky with the wood chipper. Curiously, the wood chipper shot out his penis intact. Perhaps as some ironic tribute to penises everywhere. I guess, in retrospect, I should feel very fortunate that I've not fallen around a penis or a wood chipper. Mud is not a life changer.

My partner at Shyster and Shyster is Janet Shyster. She is the second Shyster in

Shyster and Shyster. Darwin Scott Shyster, better known as Shyster Mike to his victims and federal prison inmates, is her recently estranged father and the founder of the tax preparation business. He created the business from scratch as a graduation gift for Janet. As far as anyone can tell, Shyster and Shyster is the only reasonably legitimate endeavor the man ever undertook. At least it was the only asset the authorities left when they confiscated Janet's entire life. They took her family home, the vacation property in the mountains and the one on the beach, the financial investment business that was aptly named Mo' Money because it made Shyster Mike mo' money than he knew what to do with. Mo' Money was mostly a payday loan company that doubled as an income tax refund advance company, but more on that later. Needless to say, charging a thirty-percent upcharge is a lucrative venture—until you get caught scamming little old ladies out of their pin money, better known as six and seven figure retirement accounts.

Legal fees ate up so much of Janet's resources that she was forced to take a new partner, and I was so determined to turn my life from a clusterfuck into something meaningful. I knew we could grow Shyster and Shyster from a nice little neighborhood business into a multi-billion-dollar conglomerate. A place where no one ever falls face first into the mud, and penises and wood chippers are kept at bay well out of reach of my body parts. First, we must do the impossible. We must navigate the exciting and dangerous terrain of the American taxation system while fighting off the brutal attacks of our biggest competitor—SRB. SRB, as far as I am concerned, stands for Shameless Rat Bastards.

Chapter 1: Oh, Boys

"Oh, boys!" I called out the open conference room door toward the prison gray cubicles. On the other side of the wall, Shyster and Shyster's tax season interns, Andrew Ren and Henry Stimpy, shared dual workstations.

Andrew Ren loped around the cubicle wall and skidded through a wide turn into the conference room. His dark hair fell into a wave across bright blue eyes. He reached up and wiped the locks out of his eyes with the back of one hand, his hand switching back across his face to catch the dribble below his nose, like no sane person couldn't tell what he was doing. Andrew was a twenty-seven-year-old perpetual student who couldn't stand still if his life depended on it. Even now, he twitched and jerked as if he were a rodent vigilantly taking in every detail at one time. If he had a tail, it would have been erect and fluffy with anticipation.

Andrew opened his mouth to speak, but Janet, always at the top of her game, tossed him a banana nut muffin before word one escaped him. We both choked back a giggle when he grabbed the muffin with both hands and nibbled on it squirrel style. He was a sight to behold as he sat back on his haunches in a swivel chair that I knew looked more comfortable than it really was. The chairs were uncomfortable by design. The goal of the conference room was to conduct private business with more than a couple of participants in swift order, so that we could get back to our real business—making money.

An insurmountable amount of time passed before his shorter and more rotund desk partner shuffled into the room. Henry Stimpy wore his typical colorblocked sweater that resembled a Bill Cosby garage sale leftover. The sweater was the only colorful thing about the old man, though, unless you considered gray and white as colors. At eighty-two, Henry reminded me of a slug. At times, I thought a fast forward replay of his entire workday would be the only way to tell that Henry moved at all. If he weren't Janet's uncle and cheap labor, I would have fired him the first day. Now I saw him as having a purpose that few others were equipped to fulfill, so I tolerated him, but more on that later.

"Catch," I said.

I tossed him a muffin and watched as it bounced off his forehead and splattered on the floor.

"Lolla! That wasn't very nice," Janet chided as she cleaned up the downed muffin and eased her uncle into a chair. "Henry is motion impaired. If he had caught that, we could no longer count him as disabled and qualify for the federal Equal Employment Opportunity tax credit incentive. You know how important those credits are to our bottom line. Why last year alone, it meant the difference between vacationing in Nantucket and the Bahamas."

"You're right, I'm sorry. I couldn't resist," I said as I sat a bran muffin in front of Henry while Janet tied a bib around his neck. Henry's wife Henrietta made the bibs herself. This one was beautifully embroidered with lips, teeth and read "Bite Me!"

"Before we begin talking about new business, does anyone have any old business they would like to address?" I asked.

"Oh, oh, I do." Andrew Ren raised his hand high in the air while bouncing in the seat like a bunny rabbit on steroids.

"Yes, Andrew?"

"Ms. Brigida, I was wondering...I mean...would it be possible...I mean my mother said I should tell you that calling me a boy at my age is kind of, ya know, sexist, and maybe you could not. I mean..." He cleared his throat and started over in an octave lower voice, "Henry and I are men. We would like you to stop referring to us as boys. It's demeaning. Please?"

"Andrew, I know you haven't been in the real world long. After all, being a professional student takes a lot of time and energy, but you should probably realize by now that what you learn in college is theoretical. What we do here is real world application, and in the real world—at least in the Midwest—bosses are called by Mr. or Ms. and subordinates are referred to as girls or boys. It's a term of endearment that doubles as a socially acceptable reminder of your station in the firm. Ms. Shyster and I are bosses. We make the rules, and you, as unpaid interns, are children and subject to our every whim."

Janet, as the ever-vigilant defender of all things legal, jumped in, "Calling you boys has absolutely nothing to do with sex or age discrimination, honest. If you are ten or..." Janet motioned toward Henry, "...eighty-two, we treat you the same. We'd be happy to refer to you as a girl if you want! I have the forms right here somewhere that officially outs you as a transgender." She started digging through the perpetual stack of papers that she carried with her everywhere. "In fact, if you are willing to make it official, I think that qualifies us for a new tax credit!" Her face lit up like a toddler on Christmas morning.

Andrew shrank back into his chair until his lanky form looked more like a melted gummy than his normal rodent self. He stammered and stuttered a denial in true homophobic style while firmly shaking his head back and forth, his complexion fading from pasty geek to goth white.

"And what about you, Henry?" I asked, more than ready to finish up this line of discussion and move on to something more lucrative, like making money to fill the business coffers and my private Me bank account, the account where I secret away funds for my never before revealed goal of—

Henry squeaked a response I chose to take as acquiescence to my explanation and as a request that we move on with the meeting.

"Fine," I said. "As you know, next Tuesday is January first. That means we open the doors at 12:01 a.m. I need you both in here early to greet clients, make coffee and look pretty while Janet and I stockpile completed returns."

Andrew spoke as if the words were bitter in his month, "The IRS isn't even accepting returns for another month. Do we really have to give up our New Year celebration for...for...work?"

"Yes, we do. SRB opens the filing season January second, so we have to get a jumpstart on them and lock in as many filing fees as we can," I said. I kept thinking about all the drones who returned to SRB for tax services year after year like ...umm drones...who do the same thing over and over again just because it is familiar. Besides, doing something new that might be good for them would take extra effort. If we are to gain any market share whatsoever over our biggest competitor, we have to get the jump on them."

Andrew countered, "But employers don't even send out W-2's until the end of the month. How will you complete returns without withholding forms?"

"Easy, we fill out the tax returns using pay stubs. We get paid. When the clients receive their wage and income statements from employers and banks, we'll file amended tax returns for them and earn another filing fee. In effect, we earn double the money from each client."

"Isn't that kind of shady?" Andrew asked.

"Not at all," said Janet. "There is nothing in the regulations that prevents us from maximizing our profits from each client as long as we ethically complete the returns to the best of our ability and warn clients that they may require an amended return. I checked. Twice."

I nodded. "It's pretty common in the business, Andrew. It's more of that real world application stuff that you don't learn in college. Kind of like reading, paying taxes and parenting. Just trust us."

Kids. They were all energy and eagerness and had no idea what to do with it. At Andrew's age, I was probably the same way. I had no idea yet just how much gray area surrounded most business decisions. I thought everything was black and white, just like the answers to a test. Either you got it right or you got it wrong. Boy, was I wrong. The world was full of individuals and companies who devoted their entire existences to discovering all those gray areas and profiting from them. These companies based their business plans on staying just one thin hair on the right side of the law. To compete, to stay in business at all, for that matter, the average small businessman had to do the same, to skirt illegal activity as closely as possible without crossing that line. Just ask Shyster Mike. He danced the dance for almost thirty years before he slipped. Well, in his case, it was more than a slip. He fell off a cliff with no parachute. At least he didn't fall on a penis, as far as we know...so far.

Chapter 2: It's a Sign

"I can't believe it! Those Shameless Rat Bastards stole my sign!" Janet stomped off the length of the office and then stood with her hands on her hips, her legs spread wide. She reminded me of a gunslinger squinting against the noonday sun as he waited for the sheriff to draw. "What do you intend to do about it?"

I sat my laptop bag on my desk and took a cleansing breath. Nothing like starting the day with problems before I've had a chance to sit down.

"What are you talking about?" I asked.

"You know I hired Jake and Maxi to put up signs to promote the business all over town, right?"

I nodded. Jake the Snake was our part-time debt collector. Maxi was his sidekick, or maybe he was her sidekick. I'm not sure. They were an odd couple who kept to themselves, but they were good at what they did and so polite, too. Jake called me Ms. Lolla. Jake and Maxi were always open for new projects whether the projects were related to collections, marketing or just plain gofer work. Their kind of competence was hard to find. If they had any experience in preparing taxes, I would hire a dozen Jakes and Maxis.

"Well, I had them put up an extra-large sign at the back of our lot so the commuters driving down the interstate can see it. This morning the sign was gone. Maxi said someone had ripped down half the signs Jake and she had put out around the neighborhood. The signs didn't even make it overnight before they disappeared. Those Sorry Rat Bastards..."

"Shameless Rat Bastards," I corrected.

"Thank you. Those Shameless Rat Bastards are sabotaging our advertising campaign. I worked hard on designing those signs. What with all the glitter and stickers and hand lettering. What do you plan to do about it?"

"Why is it up to me to do something about it? They were your signs."

Janet blinked and paused as if it never occurred to her that she could do something about it herself. I imagined taking care of problems was something her father always did. Now that I had replaced him, in her mind, I was on the hook for problem solving. I stayed silent and let her think about it. Janet was a solid ten on the intelligence scale but overprotected by Shyster Mike. I didn't want to push her into a role she wasn't ready for, but honestly, with tax season just around the corner, I didn't have time to spend on signs. I had bigger fish to fry like television commercials!

Before she spoke again, small children grew into men, trees lost leaves, my new cell phone became an out of date piece of trash. I may have lost a few brain cells as I tried psychically to convince Janet she could take care of the sign problem.

"I'm going to put out a new sign, but this time I'm going to make it out of plywood and bolt it to four-by-four posts. I'll need extra money to have the posts sunk into cement, and I want floodlights and a security system. If they take this sign, I want evidence I can use to prosecute the thieves. Those rat bastards will learn not to mess with me."

"No to the security system. It isn't in the

budget. You can have the cemented posts and the floodlights."

"I'll take it out of my salary."

"Fine, but I want to see the receipts."

That settled, I had time for coffee and to go over my lines one more time before the camera crew arrived. When I had decided to film a commercial, I had brought in a standing mirror because everyone knows the only way to make the best impression is to practice your lines before a mirror. Every day for the last thirty days, I had practiced, at first without a script. I wanted to figure out how to stand, to smile and from what angle I should stage my television debut. I finally settled on leaning against the front of my desk and aiming for a friendly, strong, political campaign approach. If I'm not moving, there is absolutely no chance I will fall into mud, on a penis or into a wood chipper, right?

I then added my script. The same script I wanted to practice just one more time before the big event, give or take a few dozen edits to fine tweak the message. I straightened my suit jacket, checked my hair and makeup in the mirror, posed as I had dozens of times before with my ass against the edge of my desk, my legs crossed at the ankles, my fingertips pressed easily into the edge of the desk.

"Hello. My name is Lolla Brigida. We here at Shyster and Shyster understand how complicated filing your taxes can be— way too complicated to do alone. We also know how hard you worked for your money, the same money the IRS has kept for a year already. You don't want to wait anymore, and you don't have to..."

And that's when it happened. I raised my hand to point at the mirror and fell. In the process, I somehow twisted around and slammed my chin into the edge of the desk. Pain seared through me as my teeth pierced my lower lip. I vaguely remember crying out before the lights went out. I must have passed out because I awoke in the hospital—three weeks later—with a concussion, twelve stitches and sneezing. Someone had placed a floral arrangement that included eucalyptus next to the bed. I'm allergic to eucalyptus.

Francine Zane

Chapter 3: Y'all Come In, Ya Hear!

I couldn't believe what I was seeing. Henrietta Stimpy, Henry Stimpy's loving wife, on TV, stirring something chocolaty with a wooden spoon in a bright pink mixing bowl. She had teased her hair to within an inch of its life. She wore a housedress that encompassed every color known to man. In the background, a pile of dirty dishes towered out of the sink. I begged to awaken from this nightmare before I spotted a lit cigarette or a liquor bottle. The reality was worse. She spoke.

"I'm what y'all would call a domestic goddess. I can bake, clean, change dirty diapers and dress out a 'coon..."

I felt lightheaded.

"What I can't do is prepare my own tax return. I leave that to the girls down at Shyster and Shyster..."

My head fell into my hands as I envisioned dollars flying away from me by the fistful.

Henrietta pointed the spoon at the camera. Chocolate batter dripped on the counter in front of her. "Y'all come on down on Wednesdays or Fridays, and I'll bake y'all a cake."

"She's from New Jersey, isn't she?" I asked Janet with my head between my legs to keep from hyperventilating.

"Yeah, but she decided southern is more friendly."

"And uttering the word 'coon' with a southern drawl? Was that more friendly too?"

"I suggested she refer to doing laundry, but Henrietta didn't want to be a one-trick pony."

"But coon!" I couldn't take it anymore. I jumped up and confronted Janet. "Do you have any idea how many ways that can be interpreted, especially by the African American crowd? We may be run out of town." Perhaps I could move to Montana and take up goat ranching. Running away to Montana had been my fallback plan ever since I wrote a paper about the state in the sixth grade. If I couldn't get lost in that much space that far away from anyone I knew, everything was hopeless.

Janet waved me away. "Don't be ridiculous. Why half our clientele is black. We've had to hire two more full-time tax preparers and a part-timer on Wednesdays and Fridays. And Henrietta is doing a guest appearance on *Hunter's Weekly* to show everyone how to dress out a raccoon. She's even been offered her own cooking show on the Food Network, but I'm not sure she plans to do it."

"Why not?"

"She said it would take her away from Henry too much."

"But she could promote Shyster and Shyster on national TV and get paid for it."

Janet nodded. "I suggested that. She said she would think about it if they would film the show in her own kitchen between episodes of *People's Court* and *Jeopardy*. Then she has to pick Henry up from work. He can't drive because he can't remember the way home anymore, or how to use a turn signal, as I recall."

"We would have to hire someone new to clean the office, I suppose," I said. Henrietta usually cleaned the office on Wednesdays and Fridays. It was her way of getting out of the house while keeping an eye on Henry, and it meant free labor for us. She insisted Henry wouldn't feel right about her holding a real job and refused to take money for her cleaning duties.

"Why? Couldn't we make Andrew do it? Isn't that what interns are for?"

"I suppose. He jumps around all over the place anyway. We could just tie a duster to his belt loop." I could just picture him with one of those rainbow dusters flying around after him like a gay pride squirrel's tail.

"Well, it's settled then," I said. "Andrew will do the cleaning, Henrietta will do the cooking show and you can drive Henry home for work."

"Now, wait a second," Janet said. "I'm in charge of signs. You are in charge of television advertising, remember?"

"I thought you settled the sign problem."

"No," Janet pouted. "When they couldn't steal the new sign, they painted over it. It now reads, *Shyster and Shyster, closed for business.*"

"Really? Did you catch who did it on the security camera?"

"No. They had on Richard Nixon masks and dark clothes. All I can tell you is they were men or flat-chested women."

"Well, at least, that narrows it down." I assumed we could eliminate aliens and small children from the list. "Fine, then Jake and Maxi can take on sign duty along with collections."

Francine Zane

Chapter 4: Long Live the Sign

My name is Jake. My friends call me Jake the Snake. My enemies don't call me. After me and Maxi get done with them, they can't call nobody, at least in the old days. Ms. Lolla and Ms. Janet ain't so fond of carnage, so we be practicing a more kinder, gentler brand of collections. Maxi won't even let me slap deadbeats around most days, but things may change now. Ms. Janet is ready to bust a gut over this sign sabotage. Now they done gone and painted over her favorite sign. Now me and Maxi is gonna take over sign duty. I can't wait.

I straightened my tie and pulled my fedora down at an angle. One last look in the mirror, and I smiled. Damn. I still got what my momma gave me.

"Maxi, you ready?" I called to my roommate.

"Yeah," Maxi called back.

I opened the bedroom door, walked out

into the living room, and blinked my eyes shut at the vision before me.

"Damn it, Maxi, you said you were ready."

"I am ready, you moron," said the woman standing in the middle of the living room with her skirt hiked up as she strapped a lady's pistol to her thigh.

Standing barely taller than a kindergartener, Precious Maxwell, better known as Maxi, wore a perpetual grimace on her face. I'd ask her one time—just the one time, since she'd almost gutted me for asking—why she was such a mean midget. All I'd learned was not to call her a midget. Another time, I ran into her at the High Tide bar with another little person who turned out to be her baby sister, Savannah. I learned more from Savannah in the ten minutes it took Maxi to find the bathroom and round up three more drinks than I had from Maxi in the five years we'd been partnering up. Savannah said Maxi was their father's favorite punching bag right up until she took a butcher knife to his junk one night while he was sleeping. By the time he got out of the hospital, Maxi had moved Savannah and her mom out of the city.

From then on out, Maxi was the man of the house, and the good Lord have mercy on any man who came near any of them.

Ya gotta respect that kind of woman.

Me? I had it easy growing up compared to Maxi. My momma was a good cook. Kept me clean and in school until I was old enough to run numbers. Daddy wasn't around much. When he was, he was always in a good mood, laughing and giving us kids presents. Not sure exactly what he did, but he smelled good and wore shiny shoes. He got me my numbers job. Didn't see him as much after that. Momma stopped talking about him and got mad when we did. I used to think he was a mafia boss, you know, back in the good days when the family really meant something. Don't matter much now. I'm fifty-seven. He'd be long dead.

"What's the plan, Maxi?"

"Scope out SRB, then sit tight at the sign tonight. See if they come back."

I grabbed a pair of brass knuckles off the dresser next to the front door.

"Should I bring the big guns?"

"Nah, these are paper pushers. One look at you, and they'll pee their pants."

Maxi looked me up and down as if I were

a mountain she was debating climbing. Compared to her, I guess I am. At six foot seven and three hundred fifty pounds, I gotta admit that most smaller men would rather back down than go up against me. Makes my job a whole lot easier.

"Think we are dressed for paper pushers?" I asked, looking at Maxi in fishnet stocking, a leather miniskirt and one of them teal push up bras thingies under a white wife-beater. You know, what I'm talking about? One of them bras that make a woman's boobs point at you. The bra matched the hair that she wore in pigtails. The pigtails stood out from her head like one of those Japan cartoon characters. The block heels on her Doc Martens added much-needed inches to her height.

"Yup."

Maxi, a woman of few words.

The closest SRB was about ten blocks from Shyster and Shyster. The tax shop was located in a strip mall wedged in between a dry cleaners and a pawnshop. When we walked in, a blue-haired grandma knitting behind a receptionist desk greeted us. Her shiny chrome wheelchair immediately eliminated her from the suspect pool.

"Can I help you?" Grandma asked.

"No," Maxi said as she made herself at home, strolling through the office looking into each cube.

I stayed by the door and did what I did best. I crossed my arms and looked mean.

"You can't go back there," Grandma said, pointing a knitting needle in Maxi's direction.

Grandma reached for the phone, and I shook a finger at her. That's all it took. She went back to knitting.

Maxi came back and grunted, "Nothing."

Six more strip malls, six more dead ends.

We stopped for hoagies at Sal's Deli. There's nothing like a hoagie for lunch to prepare me for a steak for dinner.

"You sure none of the SRB employees coulda done it?" I asked.

"Yup."

"Why?"

"Did you watch the security camera feed?"

"No, I thought you did."

Maxi rolled her eyes, "I did. That's why I know none of the employees I saw today matched the body type. The sign crooks were thin and tall—not you tall but tall. I saw women with middle-age spreads, men with beer bellies and petite little princesses who wouldn't have a clue how to pull off a caper like this.

"You shoulda watched the feed."

It was a fine night for a stakeout. Me and Maxi spent the afternoon replacing the sign with a new one reading:

Shyster & Shyster: You're alternative to SRB's lies.

(Bring it on, Shameless Rat Bastards)

If that wasn't a challenge, I didn't know what was.

We sat in our camp chairs behind a hedge that separated the Shyster property from the chiropractor next door. I'd brought some potato chips and nuts to crack, but Maxi wouldn't let me eat them. She said I'd scare off the perps. I think she's just mad 'cause I forgot the dip. Potato chips just ain't worth eating without French onion dip. At least I still had my Laffy Taffy to keep me company.

A little after one, Maxi kicked me. I figured I was snoring, again, but this time, she also punched me. I jerked to attention and stared out between the hedges at a couple of figures skidding down the embankment that separated the highway from the property. They looked like ninjas, staying low and looking this way and that. As they neared the sign, the floodlights made it clear that the ninjas wore backpacks. They pulled paint cans out of the backpacks and went to work on the sign.

We let them get well into disfiguring the sign before we circled around behind them. Here's where me and Maxi really differ. She likes to hit first and ask questions later. Me? I like to make 'em think. I tapped the tallest one on the shoulder. He whipped around and gaped at me like a fish out of water. From close up, I could see the black-rimmed glasses he wore on the outside of his Richard Nixon mask. I smiled and held him still with one iron grip on his shoulder.

Maxi, on the other hand, kicked her opponent in the back of the knee and watched him crumple to the ground. She then put him in a headlock with her thighs and pummeled him with tiny but powerful little fists. I should know. She'd pounded on me a time or two. It's bad enough for a guy to get beat up by a girl. How do you tell anyone that a dwarf girl took you down with one carefully placed kick?

My ninja squirmed under my grasp and reminded me why I was here. I made a fist with my free hand and pulled back to let the skinny Nixon have it when I noticed the sign. Now the sign read:

Shyster and Shyster: Home of Feminists

Huh? Maybe they meant to add something else. I didn't get a chance to ask.

"Stop! Police!"

I glance behind me and saw red and blue lights swirling behind me. Two figures with flashlights climbed down the embankment. I stared at Maxi, who stared at me, who stared at one ninja and then the other. You know that survivalist instinct that man learned two seconds after the first caveman was eaten by a dinosaur? That instinct kicked in and was reinforced by a lifetime of being on the wrong side of the law. I pushed my ninja toward the sign and took off toward my car like a lumbering ox. Maxi shot passed me and had the car door opened before I rounded the building. I hoped I'd make it to the car before my heart gave out and I landed face first onto the parking lot pavement.

My left knee felt as if the joint had been replaced by sponge. My right knee had locked up ten yards back. I now moved like Igor from the *Hunchback of Notre Dame*. My tongue felt too big for my mouth, so I let it loll out the side like an overheated dog. By the time I fell into the car seat, I saw the world through a crimson haze.

"Drive!" Maxi yelled just loud enough for me to hear over my own heartbeat.

"K-k-k-ey," I managed.

"Really? For Christ sake..." Maxi grumbled as she dug into my pocket and pulled out the keys. "If I could reach the gas pedal without my extender..." She put the key in the ignition and started the car. "...and had my booster seat..." She jumped out of the car and ran around to shut the door I'd left hanging open, then got back into the passenger seat. "I'd have left your fat ass." She threw the car into gear. "Now drive!"

We were halfway home when I slammed on the brake, throwing Maxi into the dashboard.

"Shit."

"What the—?" Maxi said while rubbing

her forehead.

"Why'd we run?" I asked.

"We always run when the cops arrive."

"Yeah, but this time, we were the good guys."

"Oh, yeah."

Chapter 5: Notice Nonsense

"Oh boy, what is on my calendar today?" I asked while sipping my Starbucks non-fat, no foam, decaffeinated, sugar-free excuse for a wake me up. I briefly considered just throwing my money out the window tomorrow.

"Well, Ms. Brigida," Andrew Ren answered. "Mrs. Hightower is waiting for you in your office, and then you have a meeting with a Darla Fishbourne and then Lizzy Deadbeat. Afterward, you promised to cover for Janet with the walk-in crowd."

"Why did I agree to that?"

"It's time for Buff to propose to her again. He's hopeful she'll say yes this time."

"Ah, that would do it." I nodded.

Janet met Buff Bronzebutt in high school. He was the quarterback, and she was rich. They made the perfect couple. Even after Shyster Mike lost all the family money, Buff continued to chase after Janet, but she's a tough cookie to crack. At last count, Buff had proposed more than fifty times. After the last time when he brought in a mariachi band, she made him promise not to propose any more often than once a quarter, till death do they part.

As it was, he drove her to work, shopped for her, bought her clothes and brought her hot chocolate and organic cookies for an afternoon snack. Why she won't marry him was beyond me. Why, if a six-foot-seven man with steel abs and a smile so bright that he put the sun to shame paid the least bit of attention to me, not only would I likely marry him, I would intentionally fall on his penis and gladly follow the family tradition of single parenthood.

Instead, I spent my time with lovely old ladies like Tiffany Hightower, who can buy and sell me at their whims but can't understand the necessity of saving receipts if they want to claim itemized deductions on their inflated tax returns. I feel fortunate if my mechanic gives me a ride to work when I take my car in for routine maintenance, and the last time a man bought me clothes, I was five. Uncle Huey wouldn't stop the car, and I wet my pants. Mom made him buy me new pants. The pants were pink. I hated pink.

I took a final swig of my non-coffee and tossed the empty cup. "Boy, bring our guest tea," I said before opening the door.

"Mrs. Hightower, what a pleasant surprise! How are you this fine morning?" I asked with the same smile on my face that I reserved for winning the lottery, which in a way, I did when I convince Mrs. Hightower to do business with Shyster and Shyster.

"Lolla, really? Do you always start your work so late in the day? How do you ever manage to stay in business?"

Mrs. Hightower looked at me through half specs perched on the end of her pointed nose. Her expression screamed that she had smelled something bad. I would have worried I had offended her, but I knew this was her normal look. If she smiled, I suspected her face would freeze, making it impossible for her to chew without food falling out of her mouth.

"Mrs. Hightower, it's not even eight o'clock. Most CPAs wait until nine to accept appointments." I sat down at my desk and interlaced my fingers.

"You aren't most accountants. You are

my accountant, and I expect more from you than most accountants."

"Yes, ma'am. Now, how can I help you today?"

Mrs. Hightower dug into her bottomless purse. Used tissues, coupons and loose change flew everywhere. She had buried her hand and most of her arm into the bag before she finally pulled out her prize.

"I got this in the mail from the IRS," Mrs. Hightower said as she handed over a crumpled sheet of paper that looked like it came out of a dot matrix printer. As if by magic, the piece of paper turned this dour lady into another woman. She looked lost. Her eyes glazed over. Her voice softened, as if the paper sucked every last drop of confidence out of her.

If I hadn't been so familiar with the IRS and their whole archaic computer system, I might have wondered when Mrs. Hightower had received the notice. As it was, I gave her the benefit of the doubt, which paid off. The notice was dated two weeks in the future. Typical IRS confusion. I swear their modus operandi was to confuse the taxpayers so thoroughly that they wouldn't even know what questions to ask to resolve the problem. I suspect half of all Americans paid whatever amount the IRS billed them just to make the agency go far, far away. Another twenty-five percent gave up the battle after an hour or two on hold waiting to talk to a real person. That left only twenty-five percent of all taxpayers who actually received the type of service they deserved. Maybe less. After all, some of that twenty-five percent were probably deceased before their issues were resolved. Not sure the dead really count.

The notice was similar to three others Mrs. Hightower had brought in during the last twelve months.

"Mrs. Hightower, this notice says you paid more into the IRS than we reported on your tax return."

"Do I need to make another payment? I don't want any trouble with the IRS."

"No. We discussed this last time, remember? If you don't tell me about all the payments you make to the IRS, then your return gets flagged, and they send you a letter."

Mrs. Hightower nodded as if I made perfect sense. "Maybe I'd better make another payment. I don't want to pay any penalties or interest."

I shook my head and counted to twenty. I promised myself a cookie if I made it through this meeting without taking a letter opener to my wrists.

"Mrs. Hightower, promise me you won't give the IRS any more of your money until next quarter. Next quarter, I'll give you another voucher to send them with a check."

She nodded again. "Of course, whatever you say, Lolla. I'll go down to the bank now and have them make out a certified check for fifty thousand. Right now, before my payment is late. I don't want any trouble with the IRS. You're such a good girl to explain all of this to me."

Defeated, I gave up the battle. I would get the amounts from the IRS and amend the tax return. It could be worse. Now on to something a little closer to home.

"While you are at the bank, do you think you could make out a check to Shyster and Shyster? You are about six months behind in paying your bill."

"Well, of course, dear. I'd be happy to pay your bill, but I'm running a little short of funds, what with all those IRS payments you've had me make. I'll pay your bill just as soon as an annuity matures. You know I'm good for it.

"Now where is that boy with my tea?"

A piece of me died just a little bit.

Francine Zane

Chapter 6: The End Is Near

Mrs. Hightower left in a fragrant haze of baby powder and roses. I made a note to sic Jake and Maxi on her then marked it out. First, I wasn't sure Jake and Maxi were up to dealing with Mrs. Hightower. Second, she was right. She was good for it. If she died before paying the bill, her estate would be responsible for the debt, plus interest. I wouldn't find a more secure investment anywhere. Yep, Mrs. Hightower was my very own penny bank. Last, I had other plans for the strange duo. Jake would make a fine tree for my *Save a tree, file electronically* campaign. I planned to dress Maxi in a blue bird costume and have her sit on Jake's shoulder. Let's see the Statute of Liberty mascot top that.

I filed away Mrs. Hightower's notice and buzzed Andrew to send in my next appointment. Five minutes later, I began to wonder if I didn't accidentally buzz Henry instead. I buzzed Andrew again. Counted to ten and laid on the buzzer like a hooker on a fat man. Little did I know at the time just how fitting that analogy fit my next client.

I had a finger crap by the time a shrunken centurion shuffled through the door preceded by an aluminum walker. Andrew held the door open from one side.

"Sorry. I didn't realize she didn't have the strength to turn the doorknob," he said as he took her arm and escorted her to one of the visitor seats in front of my desk.

"Oh," I squeaked. I cleared my throat and tried for more fortitude. "That will be all, Andrew."

Andrew left me alone with the woman in her lacy lilac dress, matching veiled hat and, if I wasn't mistaken, the very last pair of knee-high support hose known to mankind. Her face resembled a crumpled paper bag, full of lines and texture. She sighed as she settled into the seat. Her toes just barely touched the ground.

"So, how can I help you?" I asked with

my fingers interlaced in front of me.

"My real name is Darla Fishbourne, but my customers called me Tasty Tushy when I performed on stage. I was a burlesque diva back when burlesque had real class. My specialty was a peacock dance where I ended up in little more than rhinestones, carrying a peacock feather fan. I was doing great until I fell in love and married my business manager, Stanley, who had bigger plans for me. He thought we could move to Hollywood and find instant fame. Only Hollywood didn't want me. Stanley moved us to Las Vegas after that. I did the showgirl thing for a while, but Stanley found out I was worth more money doing private shows than on stage.

"It was a slow roll downhill from there. I spent most of the seventies and eighties on my back in an upscale brothel. Stanley, on the other hand, spent most of his time managing a traveling stripper show. Not one of those girls could have been a day over twenty-five, and well, I'd seen twenty-five long before Vegas.

"At least Stanley kept coming back to me. We would have been married sixty-five years next week, but last month he accidentally swallowed my belly button ring and choked. I was mortified and heartbroken." She stopped and wiped a tear from her cheek.

"I'm terribly sorry for your loss," I said.

"Thank you, dearie. We had a good life, Stanley and I, but it isn't without regrets. It's time I start making amends." She stopped abruptly, her head nodding forward as if she had dozed off.

"Mrs. Fishbourne?" I said softly, wanting to awaken her but not to startle her into a coronary. The last thing Shyster and Shyster needed was a reputation for killing off clients, especially before compiling any billable hours.

I nervously looked for signs of life such as a twitch or the rise and fall of her chest, but I saw nothing. I rounded my desk and kneeled beside her. I didn't want to touch a dead body, but I couldn't think of any other way to assure myself of her condition. My face screwed up into a grimace. I said a silent prayer, and then it dawned on me that I was the boss. I didn't have to do anything I didn't want to. Projects like this were exactly why we hired interns.

"Oh, Andrew!" I yelled.

Tasty Tushy—I mean Mrs. Fishbourne—snorted and showed signs of life simultaneously to Andrew storming into the room as if an entire hill of killer ants were on this trail. I made a mental note to double his salary of nothing. It was the least I could do.

"Sorry, did I fall asleep?" Mrs. Fishbourne leaned back in her seat and away from me.

On my way back to my desk, I made a mental note to pop a mint. "I think so. Are you okay now?"

"Yes, yes. A five-minute nap here, ten minutes there, and I'm good to go. It's just harder to realize when it's nap time, dearie."

"No worries, but I am at a loss as to how I can help you," I said.

"Oh, yes. Why I am here. I guess that would help. I am here because I have never filed a tax return. Stanley didn't believe in taxes, so we invested our money in antiques. Now we just sell off pieces for cash as we need it. But now that he's gone, I'd like to do my part to reduce this national deficit I keep hearing about on CNN."

"Really?"

"Yes, dearie. This nation of ours has

been good to me. Not many women my age can say they are still living on the money they earned as a prostitute. It's my way of giving back for all the marriages I broke up, all the STDs I passed on and all the little boy wet dreams I caused."

"Really?" I said again for lack of anything better to say. I looked around the room for the hidden cameras. Why me? Most normal people spent a lifetime trying to avoid paying more taxes than they had to, and here I had back-to-back clients who were ready to give away perfectly good greenbacks to the same establishment that had a reputation for poor money management.

I bit back the temptation to tell her to write out a check to me, and I would take care of everything for her, then invest the money in some nice solid blue chip stocks. My secret Me fund would quickly grow from small potatoes to county fair winning pumpkin sized. I could trade in the Starbucks non-fat, no foam, decaffeinated, sugar-free excuse for a wake me up for a champagne mimosa. Best of all, I could have a clumsextomy and stop landing face first in the mud.

I blinked back the dollar signs flashing

before my eyes and got practical. How much could an ex-prostitute really be worth?

"What did you have in mind, Mrs. Fishbourne?"

"I'd like you to file twenty years' worth of returns for me. That's as far back as I have records. Can you do that?"

I fought back the urge to say *really* again.

"Mrs. Fishbourne, if you take twenty returns to the IRS, you will be letting yourself in for a world of hurt. First, I'm not even sure the IRS would know how to process returns for that long ago, but the minute you do file those returns, they have the right to assess twenty years' worth of penalties and interest. That is a lot of penalties and interest."

"But I have all my business receipts..."

I nodded. "Yes ma'am, but if you didn't have any withholding taken out of your earnings, you would likely owe a lot of money, an awful lot of money."

Mrs. Fishbourne looked perplexed. "What do you suggest?"

"I could reasonably see filing the last five years."

"How about fifteen years?"

"Seven," I countered.

"Ten. Final offer," Mrs. Fishbourne said. "And I'll throw in a nice Chippendale desk. Yours is a knockoff."

"Done!" I said, jumping up from my desk to shake her hand.

"Very good. Send that nice boy around to my place tomorrow with a very large truck. Now I must be going. I have a photo shoot in an hour for next year's *Sexy Grannies* calendar."

Chapter 7: Sleazy Lizzy

With help, Mrs. Fishbourne vacated my office moments before a skinny woman with stringy blond hair and an unlit cigarette dangling out of the corner of her mouth barged in. She carried an infant in her arms and held the hand of a snotty-nosed toddler, who held the hand of a snotty-nosed preschooler, who held the hand of a nose-picking elementary school kid. From mom to the infant, they all wore matching foam flip-flops, even though it was a brisk January morning with temperatures bordering on icy.

"You got a nursery here somewhere?" The woman I assumed was Lizzy Deadbeat asked.

"Are you Lizzy Deadbeat?" I asked.

"Yeah. You got a nursery or somethin'? These kids won't sit still no time."

"No, I'm sorry."

She shrugged. "It's your loss. I'm not

51

payin' for nothin' they break. Just sayin'."

"We will hurry. Have a seat." I motioned her to a chair.

"Mikey, you take the kids over there and play quiet." Lizzy handed the infant to the nose picker and pointed him toward my crystal figurine collection.

The pair of glass lovebirds shattered just from being in the proximity of children. I blanched. My office had never seen children before, neither had my home for that matter. I didn't have anything against children, but really all I knew about them, I'd learned from *Home Alone*. I quickly came up with a plan.

"You know, your kids would be more comfortable in the outer office. I can have one of our interns watch them while we talk. Will that work for you?"

"Hell yes."

And that is how Henry became the official Shyster and Shyster babysitter.

"Let's get down to it," Lizzy pulled a wad of cash out of her purse. "I have money. I want you to file my tax return and add all four of 'em kids."

"Your kids?" I have to admit, I was a bit confused.

"Well, they are now! I bought them lock, stock and Social Security number. I want some of that free money the IRS gives out for having kids. I can't have any myself. No eggs or something, so I bought four. And I'd like some of that child support, too. I'll need to feed these brats so I can claim them again next year. No point in thinkin' small."

I had to give her credit for not thinking small.

"When did you buy your children?" I asked. I couldn't recall an IRS code that against claiming purchased children, provided she could show proof that she supported them for more than six months out of the year.

"I got the last one on the way here. The tall one—what's-his-name? His momma was a tough bargainer, but she finally gave in when I threw in a carton of cigarettes."

"Mikey."

"Huh?"

"His name is Mikey," I said.

"Whatever."

"Well, you can claim them next year, and if you legally adopt them, you may qualify for a significant Earned Income Credit and Adoption Credit."

"Next year! I'm not waitin' till next year. I want my money this year," Lizzy said. "I'm gonna use it to buy more children!"

"I'm afraid you don't understand," I said.

"What is there to understand? If I can prove the kids lived with me at least six months, I get to claim 'em, right?"

"More or less, yes, but you said you just bought these kids."

"I also said I bought 'em lot, stock and Social Security numbers. That includes forged documents showin' I had 'em at least six months. I ain't stupid, Ms. Brigida."

"I never said you were." I schooled my face to impassivity. It wasn't my job to judge. My job was to make Shyster and Shyster money and to offer services to whoever could pay for them. Lizzy could afford me. I'd seen hundreds in that fistful of bills, but that little bit of me that had gone to Sunday school, who loved my mother and hated the evil stepsisters in *Cinderella*, that part of me wanted to do bad things to this woman. That part of me wanted to sell her to a fat rendering plant right after I personally scratched her eyes out. I looked at my fingernails and remembered how much my manicure cost me—almost as much as I would earn during this meeting.

"You might not have said it, but I know what women like you think of women like me. You with your college degree. You don't know how it is comin' from nothin', havin' nothin', then the government wants to take away what little bit of money we do make. I'm just takin' what is due me. You can help or not. Makes no difference to me. SRB said they'd do it, only they want a bigger cut of the return than I'm willin' to share."

Damn. She played the Shameless Rat Bastard card. I could have stood up against anything but the Shameless Rat Bastards! Now I had no choice. If Lizzy could forge up the right paperwork, I'd have to take on the work. I know! I'll pass the actual work off to someone who didn't know the kids were commodities, someone like Janet. Janet would believe anything! And after Lizzy paid her bill, I could anonymously get help for the kids. Yeah, that would make me some kind of hero, right? Right. Yeah, and the corns on my feet might transmute into big ol' chunks of gold.

"No, no, we will prepare your return. I will arrange for my partner to make time for you as soon as you have the paperwork together, but you have to promise me to keep your child purchasing to yourself. All Ms. Shyster needs to know is they are your kids."

"Well, that's more like it! Now how about that child support?"

"Lizzy, the IRS doesn't pay out child support. That is something one parent gets from the other parent. The state manages child support."

"These kids don't got no daddies. The state will have to pay me and collect from the wind."

"It doesn't work that way."

"You sure? My Aunt Sally collected child support for me until I turned eighteen. I never did see my dad."

"Yeah, I'm pretty sure."

"Then how am I supposed to keep these kids fed for the next year?"

"What about the money you showed me?"

"I took out a payday loan. The TV said I'd get a refund in three weeks. Figured it'd be enough to pay off the loan, and you. The rest, I'm spending on a boob job and two more kids..."

Either she had no idea how much plastic surgery cost or kids didn't cost much more than the carton of cigarettes Lizzy had thrown in on the purchase of Mikey.

"...and then next year, I'm gonna itemize the cost of the boob job and get even more government money."

"It doesn't work that." The blue haze of déjà vu settled in.

"Ms. Brigida, if you keep tellin' me that, I'm gonna start wonderin' what that fancy college of yours taught you. Maybe you should just stop talkin' right now."

Maybe she was right. I nodded and watched as she got up and skipped to the door, her long blonde hair swaying from side to side. I could have sworn I heard her humming the theme song to *Cops*.

Francine Zane

Chapter 8: Fairy Charming

I downed a shot of the liquid courage I kept locked up in the office safe for just such occasions. I'm not nearly the idiot Lizzy thinks I am, nor so callous as to think those children were any better off with Lizzy than parents who would sell them. I had an ethical obligation to do something, and I would. I was just riding that line between success and failure. I had to make this work. I had too many people depending on me—Janet, Andrew, Jake, Maxi, Henry, Minnie, Mickey, Donald, the Three Musketeers, my dead Uncle Huey, the guy who mowed my lawn, my hairdresser, Macy's, the cat I hoped to someday own and ignore.

I was still looking for a place to hide the minibar-sized empty bottle when music outside my office window demanded my attention. No need for the natives to realize I'd taken up drinking to deal with the crazies. No need for the crazies to know they were getting to me. I dosed the liquor breath with Tic Tacs. I ended up stashing the empty bottle back in the safe. Better to be *safe* than sorry, right? Hehe.

My office window overlooked what was once the back parking lot where no one parked unless the front lot was full. Now it looked like a Renaissance fair. Lords and ladies lined a red carpet leading from a fairy princess bedazzled carriage pulled by two white horses to the door. A quartet of musicians played something liltingly beautiful. A banquet complete with a roasted pig with an apple in its mouth awaited. A jester pulled a floral bouquet from his sleeve and presented it to a little girl who paused from her task of dropping white rose petals along the carpet. And then there was Buff. Even in tights and a curly blonde wing, he stood out as a man among men, head and shoulders taller than most of the royals below me. The sun glinted off his shiny white teeth. Beside him stood his faithful page carrying a crown on a gilded pillow. Crown—ring—seemed fitting and unique in this day and age.

This was truly a picture from a fairy tale.

Janet had to say yes this time!

The door crashed open and then shut behind me. I twirled around to find Janet leaning against the door, struggling to keep it shut long enough to lock it.

"Help me!" She said.

I put my shoulder into it, and between the two of us, we kept the minions on the other side from coming in long enough to lock it.

We relaxed against the door. I turned to Janet. "What is going on?"

"Really?" Janet asked. "You didn't see that ridiculous set up outside?"

"It's not ridiculous. It's sweet. What girl wouldn't want a fairy princess marriage proposal?"

"Well, me for one!"

"He loves you."

"And I love him," Janet said.

"Then what is the problem?"

The pounding on the other side of the door picked up again.

I pounded back. "Knock it off!"

And then there was silence. I walked Janet over to the couch no one ever used, and we had a seat.

"Seriously, what's the problem? He

seems like a great guy, and you admitted you love him."

"I do love him. I have since we were kids, but I just can't bring myself to say yes, especially now, after all that has transpired."

"You mean with your dad?"

"No, oh God, no! Dad has nothing to do with this. I screwed this up all by myself."

"It can't be that bad…"

Tears streaked Janet's cheeks. "Yes, it is. It's horrible."

I gave Janet an awkward hug. We were partners but not friends, not really. Sure, I knew she preferred cashew chicken to General Tso's chicken, her favorite color was blue and that she had a severe allergy to anything plaid, but that didn't make us friends. Not really. We never shared clothes or giggled over boys, except for Buff. We never painted each other's nails or traded gifts for the holidays. Hell, I'd never even been in her home.

"Aw, hun. Tell me about it." If she kept crying, I was going to cry too.

"It's not just one thing. It's a lot of things."

"How about the top five list?"

"Besides his name?" she asked through a pained laugh as she wiped away tears.

"What about his name?"

"Are you telling me you wouldn't mind being a Bronzebutt?"

"Well, yeah, but there's no reason you have to take his name! You can remain a Shyster."

Janet nodded, "...but I'd still have to introduce him to friends and family as a Buff Bronzebutt, you have no idea how embarrassing that can be, especially when they ask me if his butt really is bronze. We don't go practically anywhere anymore. It was okay when we were kids, but we aren't kids anymore."

"Surely that isn't the real reason you won't marry him," I said. If his name had been the real reason, she would have left him a long time ago.

"No, not really. The real reason is Buff's dad, Daddy Bronzebutt—you know how he made his money, don't you?"

"Doesn't he own a fitness center out south of town?"

"South, north, east and in twenty-six other areas, but that isn't how he made his money. He produced and starred in all those clench and release butt exercise videos that were so popular twenty years ago."

"Oh! I remember those. *Daddy B's Two Steps to a Firm Butt, Daddy B's You Can Have a Butt Like Mine*...weren't there a few more?"

"Yeah, *Daddy B's Tight Cheeks, Daddy B's Don't Hate Me for My Fine Ass, Daddy B's Ladies with Big Butts.* He made millions, and that was before he started the *Baby B's Clenched Cheeks, Baby B's Baby Bunmaker* and *Baby B's Bodacious Best Body Parts* videos for kids."

"I take it Buff is Baby B?"

"Oh yeah, and it gets worse."

I was kind of hoping so because so far I had no idea what the big deal was. I grew up with two women who fell on penises and an uncle who died in a wood chipper for goodness sake. In my world, embarrassing relatives were as common as lobbyists on Capitol Hill. You learned to live with them, ignore them or hide from them. Of course, it's easier to hide from them when you are an adult and can move six states away. Until then, the crazies tend to follow you around and demand attention under the guise of doing what is best for you. Uh huh.

Right...as if...

Janet continued. "When my daddy got into trouble, I was scrambling to find money for legal bills. Buff urged me to approach his dad. I put it off as long as I could, but in the end, there seemed to be no other way. Daddy B made me feel about the size of a microbe before he made me a deal I couldn't refuse.

"He told me no boy of his would ever marry the offspring of a jailbird. He said he'd always known daddy was a crook, and he thanked goodness I was no daughter-in-law of his. He made me sign a contract agreeing never to marry his son in exchange for the money I needed."

"Oh, that is just wrong. What happens if you break the contract?"

"That's the worst part," Janet said, with fresh tears in her eyes. "If I marry Buff, Daddy B will take over my interest in Shyster and Shyster, and he will tell Buff about the baby."

The dam broke and all of Janet's anguish washed down her face. All I could do was hold her for a long time and make the same comforting noises you would to an infant. By the time my shoulder was wet from what I told myself were only tears, Janet had gone through a box of tissue and the forest green carpet was decorated with crunched tissue flowers. *Tiptoe Through the Tulips* by Tiny Tim played in my head. I prayed it wasn't a sign that the crazy relatives had finally rubbed off on me.

"Now tell me about this baby. What baby?" I rubbed Janet's back.

"Right after my freshman year in college, I came back to town. Buff was here waiting for me, as he always was and is. We had a great summer—too great of a summer. I knew I was pregnant before I went back to school. Of course, I didn't tell him. He would have insisted on marrying me."

Nothing new there.

"And back then, I was still thinking that one day we would marry, but I didn't want to *have* to get married. Besides, Dad would have flipped his lid. He had married my mom with a bun in her oven. He would have been so disappointed in me, so I did what I thought was best. I hid the pregnancy as long as I could, then I arranged to take a semester off and disappeared. I gave the baby away and went back to school."

"That must have been awful," I said.

"Not really. I had a lot of time to think about it, and it was the only logical answer. To this day, my only regret is getting caught."

"Surely Buff will forgive you."

"No way."

"Oh, yes, way. Very much way. He loves you."

"You are still missing a massive piece of the puzzle. You see, Daddy B found the baby and somehow manage to adopt him away from his adoptive family. The baby is Buff's adopted brother Biff."

"Seriously? As in Biff and Buff Bronzebutt?"

Janet nodded. "Biff and Buff are father and son and mortal enemies."

"Oh no, mortal enemies!" As opposed to what? Immortal enemies? Animal enemies or maybe alien enemies?

"Yeah. Apparently Biff grew up a little wild and killed Buff's pet turtle during a drunken rage. He also freed Buff's pet moth collection right in front of a fan. The poor things didn't have a chance. They instantly diced into moth confetti. Then Biff did the unthinkable. He mixed up an energy drink for Buff using his mother's ashes and urine as a base. After he added the raw egg and kale, Buff had no idea until Biff told him...during his mother's funeral, then Biff mooned the funeral procession as they pulled into the cemetery. After we had buried Buff's mom, we went to leave and found that Biff had stolen the hearse.

"Buff swore then and there that if he ever saw Biff again, he would kill him. I can't imagine what he would say if he found out Biff was his son."

"Don't you think it's kind of unfair not to tell him? And if you told him, that would be one less thing Daddy B could hold over your head."

"You're right, but how? Certainly not now, with Buff dressed up like some ancient fop."

I stood up and offered Janet my hand. "Probably not now, but you have to at least go put him out of his misery for another three months. That should be enough time to straighten things out."

"But what about Shyster and Shyster? I can't give it to Daddy B."

"We will work out that wrinkle when and if Daddy B tries to enforce the contract. For now, suck it up and get out there, missy." I gave her my most comforting smile.

"You are coming with me."

"I wouldn't miss it!"

We opened the door to find a wall of Shyster employees and a petite Asian woman with a measuring tape around her neck blocking our way.

I could feel Janet melting beside me. I put a supportive arm around her waist and kept her upright.

"What did you hear?" I ask.

"Oh, nothing."

"Gotta get back to work."

"Just picking up a pen."

"Hearing aid battery almost dead."

"Nice lady princess got knocked up and gave away a bad baby. Now she can't get married," the mysterious Asian lady said. "Now you give her to me. I get her dressed and send her to the prince."

And with that, she whisked Janet away, leaving me gaping at a mess.

"Do I need to tell you what happens at Shyster and Shyster stays at Shyster and Shyster?" I asked and was relieved when the mumbles and head nods constituted a verbal contract, of sorts.

Fifteen minutes later, I stood behind the jester, well behind the royalty for hire, and watched as Janet emerged from the building. She wore the traditional Cinderella gown. Glass slippers peeked out from beneath a gilded hemline. Her lips were ruby red, and her hair was swept up in a chignon. The quartet played something similar to a wedding march, and Buff—the handsome prince of this little production—got down on one knee.

"Janet, I've loved you forever. Will you please be the princess in all my fairy tale dreams?" He presented her with the diamond-laden crown and waited.

And waited.

And cleared his throat.

Finally, Janet responded so softly that I almost missed the words. "I love you, but no."

And then she was gone, off like a flash toward her car, leaving behind one glass slipper as befitted any good Cinderella. Buff looked like he might cry as he watched her drive off. When would the man ever learn? He set himself up for humiliation every time he insisted on one of these elaborate proposals. Janet was analytically minded. Buff wasted all this romance stuff on her. He would have better luck if he would light some candles at home, cook a good meal and provide Janet with a spreadsheet showing the pros and cons of matrimony. If he would just show her the numbers proving marriage a lucrative venture, she would be his in a heartbeat.

Francine Zane

Chapter 9: Where's My Refund?

The phone rang. I picked it up and was greeted by, "Where's my refund!" even before I had a chance to say hello.

"One moment," I said into the receiver.

"Janet, it's for you," I yelled through the open door. "Refund call."

"Oh for Christ's sake, Lolla. You can answer the question as easily as I can."

"Yeah, but I don't want to," I said.

Janet growled at me and slammed her door. As a rule, Janet was the epitome of the cool, calm professional, but the farther we got into the season, the more hours we put in beyond the normal nine to five, the less patience Janet seemed to have. I'm sure it had nothing to do with me. I'm a dear to work with.

I picked up the phone. "Hello?"

The deep man's voice stormed my ear. "Where's my refund?"

"Sir, we are not the IRS. I can give you the number to the IRS where you can get a status update on your refund."

"Don't you think I've called that number? It still says my refund is processing."

"I'm afraid that means your refund is still processing. I would give it another week."

"You people promised me my refund in seven to twenty-one days!"

"I believe our standard contract states that normally you can expect your refund in seven to twenty-one days from the date that the Internal Revenue Service starts accepting returns, provided you fully disclosed all income, expenses and credits. Shyster and Shyster cannot be held libel if you owe money to the IRS or any other government agency. In the event the IRS takes longer than the published timeframes, Shyster and Shyster cannot be held responsible. In the event you move after filing you tax return and do not notify the IRS timely, or you close your bank account, Shyster and Shyster cannot be held responsible for the delay in receiving your refund. In the event your refund is lost in the mail, stolen, tossed in the trash by mistake, spent during a drunken rage and you have no memory of the event or you die prior to receiving your refund, Shyster and Shyster cannot be held responsible. In the event—" I paused for a breath.

I knew this clause by heart because I spent a good three weeks developing it. Yes, we provided a money back guarantee to each and every client, but we made the guidelines as tight as we could to prevent anyone from collecting on the guarantee. You should read the twelve pages of exclusions in exam issues guarantee.

"Where's my refund!" the caller asked at the top of his vocal range.

I held the phone out from my ears as far as my arm would allow and yelled back, "Sir, I have no idea where your refund is." I was getting tired of this conversation.

"You're my accountant. You are supposed to make sure I get my refund."

I counted to ten and reminded myself that he was a client. I didn't make money if I didn't have clients, then I sugared my voice for one more try.

"Sir, technically we are your tax preparers. We charge a lot less than a CPA. However, if you are willing to pay our hourly rate, I will assign someone to expedite your refund."

Silence. "How much do you charge?"

Oh goodie. Now was my chance to see exactly how much he wanted that refund. "We charge twenty-two fifty per hour up to and including the full amount of your pending refund. The fee will be deducted from your refund prior to depositing the balance in your bank account. We have thirty days from the date of receipt of the refund from the IRS to deposit the balance into the bank account of your choice. We do have a bank card option, which we charge an additional twenty-five dollars to activate, but we reduce your wait time from the thirty days to twenty-seven days."

"Three days earlier, huh? Where do I sign up?"

I transferred him out to an intern, only slightly ashamed of myself for the exchange. When would people ever learn how much they gave up for expedited service? Not in my lifetime, I hoped. The margins on expedited services were astronomical. Besides, I deserved compensation for my bleeding eardrums.

The phone rang again. Oh geez. Not again.

"Shyster and Shyster, how may I help you?" I rolled my eyes then stared at the ceiling while the lady on the other end told me her story. I wondered if the ceiling was high enough to hang myself. Then I wondered if the hanging ceiling frame was actually strong enough to hold my weight.

"Where's my refund?"

"I'm sorry. We are not the IRS. I can give you the number to the IRS where you can get a status update on your refund."

"I've already called that number twelve times today, and before you asked, I already checked the website as well."

At least that is what I think she said. Hard to hear over the TV blaring, the ringtone, the baby crying and something that sounded a lot like bacon frying.

I checked my nail polish for chips. "Uh huh, and what did you find out?"

"Hush! Go find your daddy. Shakita, flip that salt back. It's burning. Oh, huh? What did you say?"

"What did you learn about your refund?"

"The refund went out yesterday."

"And why are you calling me?"

"Well, the IRS campus is six blocks from here. If the refund went out yesterday, I should have it today. Since I don't, it must be lost."

"Ma'am, just because you live close to an Internal Revenue Service campus doesn't mean the refund was issued from that site. The IRS has locations across the nation."

"Well, that just don't make any sense at all. They'd save a lot of money if they shipped locally."

I counted to ten—twice—as I wondered how often she used the United States Postal Service. Maybe I was missing something like a special stamp for sending local mail. "Yes, ma'am. Unfortunately, the IRS doesn't see it that way. You need to allow up to ten days to receive the refund."

"Fine. I guess I'll call the bank and see if it was delivered there instead. I did provide my bank information." The background noise went up a notch as the baby screamed directly into the receiver.

"Yes, ma'am. You do that." I dabbed at my ears with a tissue. Blood splatters dotted the white paper.

The second I hung up, the phone rang again. At this rate, I would get no more work done until well after April 15. These interruptions were unacceptable. This was the height of our season. What money we earned now would carry the company until October when taxpayers with extensions of time to file would expect their returns completed. We wouldn't even start working those returns until the last minute, thereby proving just how busy our schedules are and how difficult balance due returns were to complete. The more complicated the work, the more we charged. See? A win-win situation for everyone. And then there were my bleeding ears that would require medical treatment and arduous physical therapy before they healed.

"Shyster and Shyster—" I managed before I was cut off.

"Where's my refund?" The voice sounded like the girl hadn't hit puberty yet.

"I don't know. Where did you leave it?"

"What do you mean by where did I leave it? I left my return with you," the girl said.

"I know you did, but that doesn't explain what you did with your refund. Have you checked under your bed?"

Silence. "Okay. Wait a second..." More silence.

I debated if I used the phone cord to hang myself whether the police would consider it suicide or self-defense against further torment. The charge would totally affect the amount my life insurance paid out.

The girl was back on the phone and breathless. "It's not under my bed."

"Well, I would keep looking for it. You know, a refund can't just walk off without help."

"Okay. I will."

"Call back in a week if you don't find it. We will help you file a missing refund report with the police."

And the phone rang. I stared at the phone as if it were a rattlesnake ready to strike. I picked my opening and grabbed the thing around the throat and prayed I wasn't poisoned in the process.

Before I could even raise the phone from the cradle to my ear, I heard, "Where's my refund?"

I chose to ignore the question. "Shyster and Shyster. This is Ms. Brigida. How can I help you?"

"Ma'am, how are you doing today?"

"I'm doing just fine. How are you?"

"Well, I'm a little frustrated here. I came into your office a week and a half ago. Some skinny gentleman with some sort of physical handicap that made it impossible for him to sit still..." Andrew Ren strikes again. "...he helped me file my return. He was a nice man and promised I'd have my refund any day now, but it's been a week and a half and I still don't have it."

"I'm sorry, sir. Mr. Ren should have clarified that it might take up to three weeks for you to receive your refund." I yawned.

"Well, I guess I kind of understood that, but me and my family are facing a real hardship."

"And what is your hardship, sir?"

"Well, we spent our rent money to take a trip to Hawaii—you know how important it is to have some alone time with your spouse, if you want to keep a marriage going. And then our oldest daughter had her sweet sixteen birthday party last week..."

"Please express my happy birthday wishes to your daughter," I said.

"Why thank you. For the party, she wanted a band, so we hired One Direction to entertain her guests. As you can imagine, Harry, Zayn, Liam, Louis, and Niall don't work for peanuts."

"I can imagine." I pulled out the world's

tiniest violin and began playing.

"Ma'am, what is that sound? It almost sounds like a very large car squeezing into a parking spot designed for a motorcycle."

"Close. It's the world's tiniest violin. I've never had one lesson. You can't even tell, can you? Do go on." I continued to play as he spoke.

"As I was saying, One Direction does not come cheap, and we were behind on the rent already. Now if we don't get that refund this week, we won't have money to buy the baby any diapers."

"I am so sorry to hear about all your problems. I can't stand the thought of your baby going without clean diapers, so I will tell you what I will do. Shyster and Shyster just installed a drive-thru. If you bring the baby by each time he needs a dry diaper, I will have one of our interns change his diaper."

"But what about the rest of my family? We'll be living on the streets if we don't get that refund!"

"Perhaps you should call One Direction for help."

The call disconnected, and I accidentally on purpose slipped the handset into the bottom drawer of the desk. If anyone asked, I'd swear it fell in there when I was reaching for the glasses that I don't wear. Maybe no one will notice.

I wondered who prepared One Direction's tax return.

Francine Zane

Chapter 10: Signtastic

I stared at the sign with my arms crossed. I tilted my head one way and then the other.

"What do you think?" I asked.

"Who would have thought?" Janet responded.

The Shyster and Shyster: Home of Feminist sign was now the home of the Feminists for Free Advertising's—also known as the FFA's—first sign rally. The back of the Shyster and Shyster lot was filled with women in ski caps, parkas, wool socks and earmuffs. A good many of them were accompanied by young children of both sexes. Minivans, RVs and pop-up tents filled the back parking lot. Behind us, parked along the side of the freeway, news vans lined the blacktop.

"I guess we don't need the security camera," I said.

"Not with this crowd here. I wager they

would lynch anyone who tries to change this sign."

"Not what SRB had in mind, I'm sure."

"Probably not."

"Probably meant to write feminist pigs or something."

"Or feminist forsakers."

"Feminist crooks?"

"Feminist dimwits."

"Feminist Nazis."

"Feminists sluts."

"Feminist—" And two white women with a black boy interrupted me.

"Pardon me," said the taller of the two women, well I assumed she was taller since the other woman was in a wheelchair. "Would you mind having your picture taken with us, in front of your sign?

"My name is Brandee. We're down from Alaska. I operate the first ever lesbian cross country hiking tour there. We specialize in feminist camp songs. Mick here," she patted her wheelchaired friend's shoulder, "actually lost a leg as a militant feminist. She specialized in severed penis revenge in the most painful means possible on behalf of abused women around the nation, at least until the accident."

I had to know. "And exactly what is the most painful means of penis revenge?"

"Well, it's a multi-step process, and I didn't take on the task by myself. I had lots of help. First, our group had friends in South America who kept us supplied with this teeny tiny little fish called a candiru, or vampire fish. These little buggers are attracted to the ammonia found in human urine, so I picked up the snarky abusers who were all so willing to cheat on wives and girlfriends. After a drinky dinky or two, I invited them back to my place for a midnight swim.

"It was oh so easy to get them naked, bladder filled, and in the pool with the vampire fish. Nine times out of ten, the guy pissed in the pool before I have time to slip off my shoes. Ten seconds later, the vampire fish smelled the ammonia and did what they do best. They swam upstream into the guy's penis. From the fuss the guys made, I'd say having a fish stuck up your penis is at least as painful as childbirth. So I'd let them suffer for a half hour or so before calling an ambulance. Then came step two.

"The only way to remove a vampire fish from a man's penis is through surgery, which was performed under anesthesia, only the anesthesiologist was a member of our militant group. Instead of knocking the guy out, she slipped a special cocktail into the guy that put him under just enough as to appear unconscious while it totally paralyzed him."

"Ouch, so he felt the entire thing?" I asked.

"Every single excruciating second," Mick said.

"But wait! It gets better," Brandee piped in while pointing a finger toward the sky.

"Yeah, it gets better," Mick said. "Once the miserable, malignant piece of shit passed out and the doctor's finished the surgery, he was wheeled into a recovery room where another militant feminist got her hands on him. Then the real pain began. She injected him with a drug that has never even been tested by the FDA. The drug prevented him from having an erection for a minimum of six months and made his man boobs grow at least two cup sizes."

"That seems kind of harsh, doesn't it?" Janet said.

"Oh yeah!" Mick and Brandee said in unison with smiles on their faces that rivaled those of small children everywhere when presented a double-dip ice cream cone dripping with chocolate topping, sprinkles and candies.

"But how did you lose a leg doing that?" I asked before I remembered it might not be polite.

"Oh, that. I lost it crossing the road to shop at a National Rifle Association garage sale. Some granny in a blue Lincoln plowed into me before I could replenish my supply of buckshot and rifle magazines. I lost my last two magazines hunting...rabbit."

"How—" I didn't ever find out what one event had to do with the other. I was probably better off not knowing. From behind us, questions came fast and heavy from the herd of reporters stampeding toward us.

"Ms. Shyster, how long have you been a feminist?"

"Ms. Shyster, over here," another reporter yelled. "How big is this gathering? How long did it take you to pull it together?"

"Ms. Brigida, is it true you are such a tough ass that you don't even use toilet paper, preferring corncobs instead?"

"Who said that!" I yelled, looking over

the sea of faces and cameras. Everyone ignored me.

Brandee put two fingers up to her lips and whistled. "Hey! They can't answer your questions if you don't give them a chance to speak. Show some respect."

She became a singlehanded security team, spreading her arms wide and forcing the media back until there were a good six feet between them and us. Every time someone spoke, she spoke louder in a booming voice that echoed off the mountains fifty miles away and scared small children. Eventually, she brought the mob to its knees, as meek as mice in the presence of a clowder of cats.

"They're all yours," Brandee said in an astounding Vanna White imitation.

I nudged Janet forward, and she rolled to her left and behind me. With a shove from the rear, I found a face full of microphones suddenly before me.

"Thank you all for coming and thank you to all the fine women who came out to support us. Shyster and Shyster would be nothing without the support of the community, and this community will lead us into a future of equality!"

A round of applause told me I was on the right track.

"We at Shyster and Shyster are not the heroes. These women are. I invite you to visit with them, hear their stories and decide for yourself if feminism is alive and strong!"

I clapped along with the crowd and slowly backed away as I made plans to hire more tax preparers. I glance toward Janet and could have sworn I saw dollar signs in her eyes.

Gotta love free publicity!

Francine Zane

Chapter 11: One Moment Please

I walked into the office and grabbed the mail off the counter. Bill, bill. Woot! I qualify for a small business loan at a gazillion percent interest. Bill, a coupon for a free pizza with the purchase of twelve pizzas. Twenty-seven notices from the IRS about various taxpayers. Nice. That meant repeat business. We might have to expand the staff again right before Tax Day.

Speaking of staff, I looked around and saw no one. I walked down the aisle into the cube jungle and looked left then right. Cube after cube held employees on the phone, feet propped up on the desk, eyes glazed over, video games up on their monitors. I stopped at Andrew's desk and ask for the phone. What I heard was the IRS graveyard.

Thank you for calling the IRS. Your call is important to us. Please wait for the next contact service representative. Your estimated wait time is six days after hell freezes over. Thank you for calling the...

Holy taxation, Batman! I could see my profits flying out the window. This would never do, so I headed straight for Janet's office.

"We've got to do something," I said as I closed the door behind me.

"Every one of the employees is sitting on the phone with the IRS. We don't charge enough for infinite wait times."

"Yeah, you're right," Janet said, not looking up from her computer monitor. "We are making a nice profit now, but what we earn now has to carry us through until fall, more or less. We don't have nearly enough business accounts with quarterly filing requirements and mega profitable returns."

"Yeah, I know. What are we going to do about it?"

"Charge more money?" Janet suggested.

"No. If we charge more money, we won't be competitive with the Shameless Rat Bastards."

"Hire cheaper labor?"

"How do we find labor cheaper than minimum wage?"

"Well, we can hire more interns."

"More Andrews bouncing around here

like a chimpanzee? No thanks. I value my sanity more than that."

"Well, you think of something," Janet said. "I've got my own worries."

"Like what?"

"We are finally making enough money to worry about the tax consequences. We could end up paying all our profits out in taxes if we don't watch it."

"Remember the days when we could just buy a company car and eat up all the profits before year end?"

"I don't want a company car. Daddy bought me a BMW right before he was convicted. I'm not sure where he got the money, but it was sitting in my driveway Christmas morning. I'll never get rid of that machine. Never."

We couldn't use kids. Kids couldn't be relied upon to stay on the phone, and this wasn't a day care center. Although, running a daycare center would be a nice second income stream. Second income stream...second income stream...how to make waiting on the phone a second income stream, and then it hit to me.

"Janet...does Henry still have to recharge his pacemaker."

"Yeah. What did you have in mind?"

"You'll see..."

"Henry, you sit here," I helped Henry ease into the oversized recliner and fit the sippy cap over his head. You know the kind if hat with the cup holders on each side and the long straw? I slipped the straw between his lips and made sure the built in headset were plugged into the phone. The physician stood by with the pacemaker charger. If this worked, I'd solve all our problems and make the company money.

Janet dialed the IRS and punched through the menu to the infinite hold pattern that plagued taxpayers everywhere. And we waited. And we went to lunch, shopping and a late movie. Then, for a change of pace, we waited. The doctor changed Henry's full urine bag, checked his pulse—I'm not sure why, he was snoring with a slow, steady wheezing sound. Then it happened.

Over the speaker, we heard, "Hello, Internal Revenue Service. My name is Fritz Fussbudget. My ID number is 100010010201764318. How can I help you?"

That triggered the medical device, the one I had made up especially for this purpose. The device shot a jolt into Henry's pacemaker, waking him up and charging the pacemaker for upwards to thirty days.

"Hello?" Henry mumbled.

Success! I'd found the solution to the perpetual hold problem. Senior citizens. We would set up six recliners, each with its own TV, hat/headset and pacemaker charger. We would advertise in every senior citizen center for volunteers to monitor the phones, charge them fifty dollars a shot to recharge their pacemakers and all our regular staff could go back to doing what they do best— making me money.

I was a freaking genius.

Francine Zane

Chapter 12: Crunch Time

Every year, without fail, the United States government sets aside one day a year to make my life hell. No matter that it happens every year on the same day, no matter how much advertising the IRS and one million, two hundred and seventy-two tax preparers do, the average US citizen is determined to wait until the very last day, the very last hour and minute before bringing in six boxes and a handful of receipts for processing. These citizens will demand a money back guarantee in the event I screw up one little line item and ask for a discount on my bill because times are tough. I will immediately agree, hike up the fee by twenty percent, then show them a ten percent discount on their bill, as will any tax preparer with an iota of business sense.

Last minute filers are a very lucrative component in our business plan. We make "Your failure to plan, or act, is not our problem" into an opportunity. For three solid weeks, I do not sleep, at least more than three hours at a stretch.

I see nothing, hear nothing, know nothing but dollars and cents. Money coming in, money going out, money charged, money paid. Money saved. Money earned. Money spilling through the fingers of the stupid into the coffers of the government, who stupidly spend the money faster than the money comes in. I think about the money in my Me account and count down the amount of money still needed before I can actually live my fantasy of—

Damn. We even put the senior citizens to work preparing returns. Another one fell asleep in mid return. I reached for the remote and found the control button for recliner six and gave the sleeper a light jolt. The old man jerked awake and went back to work. I considered hooking the voltage up to all of the employees' chairs next year. How great was that idea?

All of a sudden my mind went blank as if someone flipped a power switch off and back on again. I blinked at my office, hardly recognizing it as my own, then I remembered Janet. Janet would know what

I was doing.

I darted across the room and slammed open the door. Rushed the two steps across the hall to Janet's office and burst in.

"What am I doing?"

Eyes red-rimmed, hair standing out in the ultimate Phyllis Diller impersonation, Janet looked at me from over a mountain of messily stacked papers.

"April fifteenth..." Janet mumbled. She continued to mumble as she went back to work, but I couldn't understand her.

"Time?" I asked.

"Eleven-fifty-five. Andrew?"

The end of hell week was near. I remembered. I remembered why I was thinking about money. Final push, final push, move dammit... And then the energy spike, the final energy spike I had in me peaked. I put every ounce of it in my last actions, perhaps the final actions I would ever take in life.

"Andrew! Run!" I screamed and collapsed in a heap on Janet's floor. Andrew Ren had prepared for this night his entire life. Dressed in a Flash costume in anticipation—yes I know, not appropriate professional attire but at this stage of the game, who cared?—Andrew whizzed through the building collecting every envelope, stuffed or otherwise, and tossed it into a USPS mail basket. Then he was gone out the door and two doors down to the post office. The man-child with never-ending energy was my hero. He dumped the basket into the bin at the front door under the watchful eye of some poor sap who had pulled after hours mail duty.

Andrew wasn't alone in his quest to beat the midnight threshold. A line of bleary-eyed zombies lined the sidewalk and post office steps. Each zombie carried an envelope and a dumbstruck expression, as if filing taxes had once again stolen his or her soul. I saw blood leaking from the eyes of a few, and one or two envelopes were at least large enough to hold the left hands missing from the arms of their owners.

I knew how they felt. My soul had been ripped out of me days ago, about the time my anxiety attack had caused Janet and Andrew to call an ambulance, but I was strong. Fake heart attack or not, I would not leave my post, not with so much money on the table in the form of unprepared tax returns. No, not I! That was for weaker mortals. I had talked the EMTs into leaving an oxygen tank with me.

I staggered back into my office and took another drag from my oxygen mask. The oxygen ran out days ago, but I felt better nonetheless. The worst was over. I considered going to the emergency room now, just in case, but I wasn't exactly sure where I'd left my soul, and without it, the hospital staff would have nothing to reattach. Besides, who needed a soul? That meddlesome thing just made you over think things and weenie out of doing what really needed to be done to succeed.

As the employees left for the night, Janet and I did the right thing. We handed each employee a nice sealed envelope. They had worked hard, and they deserved a reward.

After reading at least half of *101 Employee Rewards in the Modern Age*, written by John Ledgbetter Scrooge, we learned that the modern employee does not appreciate cash rewards, which we would have traditionally provided. Instead, they preferred words of gratitude and something they can hang up in their home or office, like a certificate of completion. Something that reminds them every time they look at it just how much their employers appreciate them.

Each envelope contained a handwritten thank you note, a gilded certificate of appreciation, appropriate for framing, and six pizza coupons to buy twelve and get one pizza free. Everyone loves pizza.

Chapter 13: Problematic Profits

"We made too much money!" Janet complained.

"If only everyone had our problem," I said from the comfort of her couch. Did you know if you are lying down, it is virtually impossible to fall? This has always been my favorite position. Staring at a white ceiling is highly underrated.

"No, you don't understand. We made enough that we are now in the tax bracket that requires we just shoot ourselves."

"Really? How did we do that?" I asked.

"Maybe it was Henrietta's commercial. Or the *Save a tree, file electronically* campaign."

"That was my personal favorite," I agreed.

"How are we going to top it next year?"

"We have a whole year to come up with that one." A long year and many nights of sleep and days of dreaming. Beginning tomorrow, Shyster and Shyster would be open on every other Tuesday and Thursday between the hours of ten a.m. and noon. Beginning tomorrow, only certain clients would receive the secret phone number, the one that rings directly at Janet's desk. We will leave the main phone line on perpetual hold.

"That doesn't solve our problem, though. What is the point of killing ourselves to make a living if the government is going to tax us back into poverty?" Janet said.

"Isn't there a loophole or something that would protect our profits from taxation?"

"You mean like a non-profit?" Janet asked as she bounced her pencil eraser against her desk.

"Or a church, yeah."

"What?" Janet asked. "Like the Taxation Tabernacle?"

"Or the Church of Perpetual Profits." Or the Church of Perpetual Prophets. I was easy to please.

"How about we play on the mention of giving Caesar what is his and call it Caesar's Fair Share?"

"No, man. That one is pure stupid." I said. I sat up and reached for a Twizzler. "I know! Praying with the Fishes!"

Janet said, "I can't buy that one. My vote is for the Taxation Tabernacle. We could have a choir."

"As long as I can have a crown and purple robes, I'm good with it."

"And a scepter. A gold one with a crystal knobby thing on the end," Janet said.

"Stained glassed windows and summer vacation camps for adults to learn tax savings tips."

I thought about it seriously for a few seconds. Why couldn't we become a church and make tax preparation a part of the normal church services provided to church members who tithe? We could build the entire church around protecting church members from the evil sins of the government. We could bless returns, perform exorcisms and hold congregation pray ins over audits. If we did it right, nothing we earned going forward would ever be subject to taxes again, especially if we incorporated the church into a commune. No more income tax or sales tax. That would be an automatic profit increase of twenty to thirty percent per year. The concept was freaking crazy. Even if we did no more business than we were doing now, we would show a substantial profit.

"Let's do it," I said.

"Do what?"

"Become a non-profit church."

"Lolla, you're crazy," Janet said.

I shook my head. "No, no, I'm not. This could work. We can make this work. We can buy one of these schools that's been closed down due to lack of funding. Convert it into a church, and hold weekly services. You know we know how to do the marketing and bring in new people."

"Did that lack of oxygen kill some of your brain cells? The IRS would never allow something like this to happen," Janet said.

"Sure, they do all the time. Have you visited some of these churches lately? They are nothing more than an excuse to network. Sermons last ten minutes. Hand shaking last fifteen. Everyone goes home feeling better about themselves with a handful of business contacts for Monday morning. We can do that, and we can do it better. As a bonus, we earn year round money to do the same thing we do now— prepare taxes and fight with the IRS over stupid shit like whether bikini waxes are legitimate business deductions."

"Taking on more business clients would do the same thing," Janet suggested.

"Business clients demand more handholding. No more six-week vacations and nine months out of the year part-time employment. If I wanted a real job, I'd still be working for someone else. Less risks."

"Less rewards, too."

"Like paying all our profits out in taxes?" I asked.

I held eye contact with Janet for a long time while I waited for her to come up with a refutable comeback. Ten minutes of silence later, I knew I had won. Ten minutes after that, we had a new Employer Identification Number. We were officially in the religion business.

Francine Zane

Chapter 14: Church of Perpetual Profits

How stupid. All these years and no one had ever thought to actually name a church something that spoke to everyone from all denominations, tax brackets, ethnicity, sexual preferences and nationality. People really seemed to respond well to the straight up honest. Besides, who can deny that mankind has worshipped profits since the first time a caveman traded a rock for fire?

The Church of Perpetual Profits opened its doors the first Sunday of July. Since Janet and I are both behind the scenes kind of people, we broke down and hired the only person we knew who seemed to like the limelight to act as the guide—other religions have ministers, priests, gurus, we had guides. Guide Henrietta Stimpy, dressed in a simple black coatdress and Mardi Gras beads, greeted visitors at the door. Her husband Henry, dressed in somber black slacks and a black sweater with a green, blue and fuchsia harlequin pattern on the front stood at her side with his hands in his pockets. Mostly he stared at his shoes while Henrietta stole the show, but Henrietta insisted on having her eye candy at her side.

And what a show Henrietta put on. "Y'all come on in!" was heard above all else. She hugged as many as she could get her hands on, waved and shook hands with the rest.

We had planned on maybe a hundred initial lookie-loos that first day. The converted school auditorium was more than large enough. The auditorium had enough seats to comfortably hold five hundred. Henrietta stood on stage in front of...what is beyond standing room only? Let me just say the fire marshal would not have been happy had he been on duty instead of sitting in the front row.

Janet and I stood in the wings sweating through everything we wore. We had put our entire cash pool into this endeavor. If this worked, Daddy B could have Shyster and Shyster. The company was worth nothing after everything we had pulled out. We had even taken a second mortgage out on the property, although the militant feminists had offered to buy it outright as a staging site for, as they put it, giving karma a little shove in the right direction.

"Now, remember," I said to Henrietta. "Right now, our goal is just to warm up people to the concept of a church that prays to profits rather than a holy deity. Make sure everyone feels like this is the church for them. Try not to offend anyone, and keep the focus off tithing. At least for now, I think. We want to play the numbers game. Get as many people as possible committed to the Church of Perpetual Profits. Hitting them up for cash comes later. Got it?"

Henrietta nodded. "Got it. When do I get my robes?"

"Hopefully by next Sunday. Had to have them special ordered," Janet said.

"You remembered the color scheme? Just like these beads—green, gold, blue and fuchsia." Henrietta rattled the beads for emphasis. "And I'll need Guide Children next time, to sit around the stage and look up at me adoringly. You promised. I don't have any grandchildren, you know."

"Yes, Aunt Henrietta, I know," Janet said. "We will get you Guide Children, even if we have to rent them."

"I know where to rent four kids," I piped

in. "Lizzy Deadbeat called just the other day looking for a way to make more money off her children, at least until she starts drawing child support."

"Are any of them girls?" Henrietta asked.

The crowd was getting noisy out front.

"Time to start the show, Henrietta. We'll talk about it later," I said.

Henrietta grabbed onto Henry's hand, and I reached out to separate them. "Now, Henrietta, we discussed this. We don't want to confuse the congregation. Henry stays back here with us."

"Oh, yeah, right, right. You'll watch over him, won't you?" Henrietta said.

"Like he was my own grandpa," I said. I gave Henrietta a final shove toward the stage, then I said a silent pray to the deity we were forsaking for success.

Don't misunderstand me. I was not anti-Christ by any means. In fact, I was baptized when I was twelve and seriously considered joining the ministry for all of five minutes. The thing was the Church of Perpetual Profits wasn't that kind of church. Think of it as a sub-church designed less with heaven in mind and more with making man's stay on Earth more lucrative. We planned to operate on the live and let live and be kind to your neighbor mentality, but ultimately, we wanted what everyone wants—money, money, money. Unlike those huge conglomerate churches, though, we didn't plan to hide that aspect of the operation. In fact, we planned to invite the entire congregation to prosper with us.

Henrietta spoke with her faux Southern drawl and the room went silent.

"Friends, thank y'all for gathering with us on this fine Sunday morning. We are blessed by such fine fellowship, and we hope we can repay y'all for yer kindness with a little spiritual upliftedness and..."

I slapped my hand over my face and groaned. This was not the sermon we had practiced.

"...knowledge about how to make the most of yer time on this world. We here at the Church of Perpetual Profits see your participation as a sign. A sign from the Lord Almighty that he believes as we do that y'all and y'all and y'all..." Henrietta pointed at people in the auditorium. "...even y'all unlucky souls in the back who crowded in late deserve better than y'all have. Y'all deserve all the riches this world has to offer.

"Now let us pray…"

"No prayers," I stage whispered at Henrietta, but she was on a roll and ignoring everything that didn't fit into her personal plan.

"Heavenly Father above us. Thank you for all the excesses we have thus far enjoy, but henceforth, you no longer need worry about our personal wealth. You can devote your time and energy to curing cancer, creating babies and welcoming our saintly departed into the pearly gates of heaven. From now on, we will take responsibility for our own success. We will lean on one another and raise our fellow brethren with us as we strive to turn hovels in the dirt into castles in the sky. We will believe in the Church of Perpetual Profits and in ourselves because we have the power of Christ within us. The power of Christ and fellowship is all we need to succeed. In Christ's name, amen."

"Hallelujah!" Someone in the back cried out.

I spotted a man in the back break dancing to what I assumed were voices in his head.

"Brother, come on down!" Henrietta

called out, and the crowd around the man parted like the red sea.

The man danced his way to the stage, then did a one-handed mount to propel him onto the stage without missing a beat.

Henrietta put a hand on his back and asked, "Brother, what is yer name?"

"My name is Carlos Hernandez but my friends call me Pussy Feet, cuz I'm so light on my feet." Carlos smiled and waved at the crowd who applauded in greeting.

"Welcome to the Church of Perpetual Profits, Pussy. What brings y'all here today?" Henrietta asked.

"I live clear across town, but when I heard the Church would teach me to make gold out of copper, I headed right here," Pussy said. "My daughter is sick and in the hospital. She needs surgery, and I ain't got no more than a few copper pennies left after paying rent and groceries for her six brothers and sisters."

"Well, Brother Pussy, we will make sure your daughter gets the surgery she needs..."

Henrietta then did the next thing I told her not to do, she took up a collection while Brother Pussy continued to dance. Janet had her wits together better than I did, though. She pulled out her android phone, pulled up a jaunty little tune and played it over the intercom system. At least now the congregation could hear the same music Pussy Feet did, or at least similar, I hoped. I made a note to hire a band and a ghostwriter for a bible. Just a couple of things we didn't think about during our brainstorming sessions, just like the unlikelihood of a full house and the inability to control anything that came out of Henrietta's mouth.

Chapter 15: Commercial Take Two

Henrietta and Henry have been married since before the invention of electricity, well almost. During that time, they have celebrated countless holidays and "just because" days. Gifts were given on those days ranging from floral greeting cards to sweaters, jewelry, perfume, vases, silk floral arrangements, boxes of chocolates, tins of fruitcake, knick knacks, lace doilies, snuggly blankets, embroidered pillows and embellished aprons. Henry and Henrietta saved every gift along with every bill, newspaper, catalog and magazine that ever entered their home. Add those to the piles of cross-stitched bibs, knitted socks, yarn balls, bins of thread and boxes of fabric that Henrietta stockpiled, and we had about two days of cleaning, trashing and boxing up for storage before we could film the commercial, but that wasn't the worse of it.

It's a fact of life that any time you cram that much stuff into one place, small, curious, hungry creatures visit, dribble here and poop there. They multiply, die and create interesting odors. Even the best pest control bombs, traps and pesticides may kill the invaders but do little to get rid of the remains. I should know. I found dozens of the things in various phases of decay.

That wasn't the worse of it. I fell through a dozen or so mostly empty boxes into what at first glance appeared to be a nest of fluffy white kittens that had somehow made it into the house—not surprising considering the couple's propensity for collecting things. Only the kittens weren't kittens. The kittens were a nest of mutated white rats with beady pink eyes and the ability to scream even louder than I did.

I did what any normal American woman would do. While screaming myself hoarse, I peed myself, did a girly dance that knocked over a stack of *Taste of Home* magazines and had a panic attack that felt like the entire left side of my body belonged to someone else. Afterwards, I passed out. I don't know about everyone else, but when I pass out, I fall. Had Henrietta's house been larger, I would have likely laid in a stupor until the U.S. people elected an albino baboon as president. Instead, Janet found me and brought me around by waving one of Henry's house slippers under my nose. I awoke wondering if I was in the coroner's office smelling fellow cadavers dipped in garlic sauce.

"No laying down on the job," Janet said.

"I wasn't," I said. "I passed out."

"Sure you did. You're not leaving me to deal with this mess alone."

I took a shallow breath and wished I hadn't then got to my feet, looking around to make sure I didn't fall on...well, you know.

By the time we were done, I figured God and I were even for pretty much everything I had done or ever would do. I could kill the next person who asked me if they could deduct both standard mileage and the cost of gasoline at the same time. God and I would still be even. I could join the militant feminists in their quest to torture every abusive man this side of the Mississippi, and I'd still have points left over to bomb a sleazy adult toy store—you know the kind with the peep holes in the bathrooms and the barely legal porn. Not one of the stores with the cute lingerie and novelty gag gifts. No, I mean the hardcore stuff that gives every man on the planet and some of the women a bad name.

I puked a little in my mouth at the thought of all the cookies I'd eaten from Henrietta's kitchen. Granted her kitchen was the cleanness room of the house, but still...

To think, the woman with this massive hoarding problem was now the spokesperson for our church—the same church where we invested all our assets. We must have still been sleep deprived and crazed from too much radiation used to warm up many weeks' worth of microwave dinners. We probably picked up syphilis from a toilet seat, too, and suffered from the dementia that may result. Nah, that didn't happen. A sexually transmitted disease on one of the company toilet seats would have meant one of us had time to actually have sex. Highly improbable.

As an afterthought, we should have just backed away from the house the second we saw what we were up against, but we still had a plan and Henrietta's promise that she would stay on script this time. Her idea of staying on script differed from ours.

"Ok, now, do you remember the script?" I asked as I watched the makeup artist shave ten years off Henrietta's appearance with an airbrush technique I'd once seen used by a caricaturist at an art fair.

"Sure, sure," Henrietta said. "I studied the lines last night."

"And you are sure we can't talk you into wearing the suit we brought you?" I asked.

"Oh, that was awfully sweet of you, but I promised Henry I would wear this dress. It's his favorite," Henrietta said.

Henry looked up from his seat in the corner, well out of camera ranged. His express was just as blank and deadpan as every other day. But Henrietta smiled at him as if he had paid her the highest compliment. Maybe he telepathically called her a bodacious babe while the rest of us were oblivious to their mental flirtation.

His favorite dress was the same one she wore for the Shyster and Shyster commercial. In the seventies, the dress might have been fashionable. It certainly would fit in with the flower power crowd better than the minister of a successful church crowd.

"Can you at least turn it around so the stains are hidden?" Janet asked.

"Well, of course, dear. Why didn't I think of that?" Henrietta said. She quickly removed her arms from the sleeves and twisted the dress around until the front was the back and the back was the front.

This was the type of loose fitting dress with a squared neckline that looked just about the same from the back as it did the front. I handed Henrietta a solid blue scarf that complemented the smaller flowers on the dress. If I squinted, I could almost believe the scarf provided just the calming touch needed to prevent epilepsy victims from going into a psychedelic seizure. I made a mental note to donate to seizure research in penance for the evil we were about to filem, particularly since the wall behind Henrietta totally clashed with the dress.

So we began filming the commercial. I kept a copy of the script open in front of me. If Henrietta missed one word or changed one phrase, I intended to stop production. Fifty-seven takes later, I fell to the floor and stayed there in a ball with my thumb in my mouth. A puddle of dribble ballooned beneath me. I hummed to myself and tried not to hear what was going on around me, but it was impossible.

Henrietta was in fine Southern New Jersey form. "Times are tough. The economy continues to drive food and gas costs up and salaries down. Why I don't know a single employer who even gives out annual cost of livin' increases anymore. Ya can't depend on anyone to help y'all out, not even your family, because they're in the same boat you are. Yer all screwed. Screwed so deeply into the ground that ya can't even see how screwed ya are, but the staff and members of the Church of Perpetual Profits are here to help. We can make sure that not only are ya never screwed again, in this life or the next, but y'all will live better than ever before.

"Why with the Church of Perpetual Profits, y'all will be a part of the biggest and most loving family ever known, and it's not that kind of bickering family that fights on holidays and hugs when someone dies. This family loves ya all the time, even when you stink from fear sweat or steal from yer kids to make rent money. We've all had to borrow from the kids, well not me. I ain't got no kids, just a niece who makes her uncle get coffee for her. Whippersnapper thinks she too good to get off 'er be-hind and get her own coffee, but we love her anyway, don't we, Janet?

"Cameraman, point that camera at my sweet Janet. She's such a good girl, most of the time. Her dear sainted mother would be so proud."

I assume the camera panned to Janet because she whimpered and dropped to her knees beside me.

"Oh right," Henrietta said. "She's camera shy. Point that thing back at me."

"I'm the Guide for the Church of Perpetual Profits. I'm the momma y'all never had. My Janet and her partner, Lolla, from Shyster and Shyster Tax Preparation, well they are the masterminds behind the Church of Perpetual Profits. While I mother you, since I don't have any kids of my own, they'll make sure what little money ya has grows into enough money to fight back against the sagging economy. Ya know? Kind of like droopy boobs fight back against a tight bra..."

The world went black and angels sang in perfect harmony.

Chapter 16: Guileless Guide Woes

"I will not approve airing that commercial! Not this time and never again," I insisted as I stormed around my office thinking of all the money we wasted.

Henrietta was beyond believable. She was a trainwreck posing as a guileless little old lady.

"Not only did she not follow the script in spirit, she made us look like a joke."

"People like jokes, though," Janet interjected from behind a women's magazine that featured a slinky, sexy model wearing an Uncle Sam hat and beard. I could have sworn I saw the same cover in Henrietta's collection, only Henrietta's magazine was from 1957. Just goes to show what goes around comes around.

"I don't want to be a joke! I want to be a retired billionaire with a handsome cabana boy and a never-ending supply of strawberry daiquiris. I want to be respected and loved and feared. I do not want to be a laughing stock, and more importantly, I do not want to be poor."

"You don't want to be poor?" Janet asked. "What about me? I am the daughter of a huge success. I didn't even know what it was to do without things until after I had my first gray hair."

"Well, that thing will never air," I said.

"Too late."

"What do you mean?"

"While you were escaping from reality, again, Henrietta approved the ad, and it aired last night."

"Why didn't you stop her?" My professional life was over. I might as well buy four children and collect child support from the IRS.

"Me! Why didn't you? Why do I always have to be the bad guy?" Janet said.

"She's your aunt."

"You hired her!"

"No, I didn't. I thought you did."

"Me?" Janet said. "Why would I hire her? She's crazy! I mean she is legally crazy. She's drawn a disability check for mental issues since she was twenty-one. If Henry hadn't taken guardianship of her, my grandparents would have had her institutionalized years ago."

"Seriously? Henry is the sane one?"

"Absolutely," Janet said.

"Then who hired her?"

"Does it really matter at this point?" Janet asked.

"Well, you fire her, and I'll find a replacement," I said.

"Not me. She's family! I can't fire family."

"What if we sent Henry and Henrietta on a trip to Florida for...say...the rest of their lives? Maybe she would forget all about the church."

Janet looked like she was thinking about doing brain surgery with no training. "That might just work. She did forget to put in her teeth that one day. Where will we get the money? We really did spend everything we have on the church."

"I know!" Let's close down the church for renovations for a month. That will give people a chance to forget and keep Henrietta away from the pulpit. In the meantime, we can put to Jake the Snake and Maxi to work doing what they do best."

"What is that? Scaring small children?"

"No, no. Collections, Janet. Collections. We must have enough deadbeat tax filers to pay for the trip."

"Oh, you have no idea! Mrs. Hightower alone owes us enough to pay off the national debt."

That made me pause. Mrs. Hightower was my emergency savings plan. If we collected from her, not only might we lose her business, there went my nest egg. On the other hand, technically Shyster and Shyster was out of business. We needed to drive her to the Church of Perpetual Profits.

"It's a done deal then," I said. "Time to turn loose the big dogs."

Chapter 17: Deadbeat Dilemma

"Jake? You ready?" Maxi yelled from the other room.

"Give me ten minutes. Twelve at most." I sat on the side of the bed spit shining my brand new wingtips. I was working on seeing my reflection in the shine of the left shoe.

I can tell a lot about a man from the shine on his shoes. That's one reason I hate athletic shoes. There's no shine. A man who keeps a good shine on his shoes takes pride in who he is, just like me. I like bein' a collector. It's a fine job. Kind of like an unofficial police officer. I make deadbeats pay hard workin' people what is owed 'em.

"Now, Jake... We don't have all day for you to primp," Maxi called out from beyond my closed bedroom door.

Nothing small about that dwarf's bark, and her bite was even worse.

"Five minutes," I gave in.

My door flew open and there stood Maxi. Precious Maxwell had changed her look for the job. This time, she was sporting a purple pixy hairdo, gray dress slacks and a white off the shoulder sweatshirt over a blind-me bright purple tank top. She wore a gray headband in her hair. Her shoes, though, oh man. I hoped we didn't have to chase anyone. Five-inch wedges on a dwarf are a recipe for disaster. For Maxi, this get up was conservative. Good news! Her shoes were shiny new. I liked that about her.

"One minute," She wasn't going anywhere. She'd left her booster seat and extenders in the Jeep, and the Jeep was in the shop. The woman couldn't see over the steering wheel and reach the gas pedal in my Caddy without help.

"Bastard," Maxi mumbled and walked out of my bedroom.

I heard the front door open and close with a bang, but I didn't get worried until the garage door went up. I wasn't really worried like I expected to hear a bomb go off. I was the kind of worried ya get when you have a new puppy and can't see it. You can't see the puppy, but ya know the puppy well enough to know it can get into all sorts of trouble if not properly supervised.

I took a final swipe at the wingtip and slipped it on. I grunted as I bent double to tie the dang thing. My gut had this way of getting in the way of tying my shoes lately. When I say lately, I mean in the last thirty years or so. I rushed out to the garage, not bothering to lock the door. The people in this neighborhood knew us, and anyone who knew us knew better than to mess with anything we own. We got this reputation for protecting what's ours at all costs.

I got to the garage none too soon. Maxi was snapping a battery pack into a nail gun and pointing it at my sweet baby Caddy's rear quarter panel.

"Maxi, you don't want to do that," I said.

"Give me a good reason not to," Maxi said.

"'Cuz you might miss and blow a tire, and that would delay us even more."

"You ready to drive, big man?" Maxi pointed the gun at my favorite body part instead.

"Yes'um." I climbed behind the wheel. When Maxi climbed in, I asked, "Do we have time for a coffee and donut on the way?"

"With sprinkles?"

I nodded. "With sprinkles."

A quick trip through the Donut Hole's drive thru, and we were well fortified for the trip across town to our first stop, a Ms. Lizzy Deadbeat. Ms. Deadbeat owed for one extensive tax return, and something labeled "special circumstances". The donuts were gone before we reached the dilapidated trailer park separating the middle to low class part of town from the dregs of hell where society's forsaken lived—the Forbidden Zone. This was the home of the druggies, ex-cons, welfare mamas and deadbeat daddies who would rather spend what little they had on something other than rent, security or child safety. This area was so bad that the cops didn't even patrol within the area anymore. They did, however, patrol the perimeter to make sure none of the inmates escaped.

I'd guess the cops' real plan was to stay out of the way and let the bad guys kill the worse guys with hopes more people within the neighborhood would die than be born or move in. Over time, only one person would be left standing, and then, the biggest and bravest of the police squads would band together and go in to kill the survivor. Then the whole area would have to be bombed, razed, burned and decontaminated before polite society could ever think about utilizing the space as much more than a garbage dump.

The only thing me and Maxi had to worry about going into the Forbidden Zone was getting back out. If I knew Maxi, she had at least two guns and six knives on her person. Me? I just carried the one semi-automatic, two additional clips and a pair of brass knuckles, but I knew I had extra firepower underneath the spare tire in the trunk. Only I didn't think we would need firepower for this trip. First, it was too early in the day for most of the scum to be awake, and second, this Ms. Deadbeat was a girl. I can handle most girls even without Maxi bein' with me as I am akin to a full-grown yeti only better dressed and less furry.

We pulled up outside a beat-up trailer house with a couple of months' worth of trash stacked at the curb. Two mangy dogs dug through the trash bags, kicking trash back from the pile. Two boys sat on the front steps watching the dogs. The older kid was picking at a scab on his knee. Both kids had runny noses and bruises on their legs.

Eh, they were boys. I always had bruises on my legs when I was a kid. If I wasn't falling over somethin', I was getting the tar kicked out of me by some other kid. That was before my growth spurt.

They looked cautiously at me and Maxi as we walked up to the house.

"Hi," Maxi said. "Is your mom home?"

"How would I know?" The oldest boy said. "She don't live here."

"Isn't Lizzy Deadbeat your mom? I heard she lives here," Maxi said.

"She ain't my mom. She lives here, though," the oldest boy said.

"Are you a midget?" The younger child asked. "I ain't never seen a midget before. Not in real life. Just on TV like in *Austin Powers*."

Maxi leaned over until she was face to face with the boy. "Don't ever call me a midget, boy."

"Don't call me a boy, midget," the boy said as he mimicked Maxi's angry face. "My name is Darnell."

The two stared at each other for a long time. I stayed put within arm's reach of Maxi. If she went after the boy, I'd have to restrain her. Ms. Shyster and Ms. Brigida wouldn't take kindly to us hurtin' little kids. I liked Ms. Shyster and Ms. Brigida and didn't want to do nothin' to upset them.

"Okay, Darnell," Maxi said through gritted teeth, her hands were clenched fists on her hips. "I'm Maxi. You call me Maxi. I'll call you Darnell. Deal?"

Wary-eyed, the boy consented and both the boy and the woman leaned back simultaneously, still watching each other but not likely to cause a scene.

"So, is Ms. Deadbeat here?" I asked, using my best kid-friendly voice.

"You mean Lizzy?" Darnell said.

"Yeah, Lizzy."

"Yeah, she's inside, sleeping more than likely. It ain't noon yet," Darnell said.

"Do you think you could go inside and wake her up for us?" Maxi asked.

"Oh, hells no! That woman is meaner than a snake when you wake her up. You want her awake, do it your own self," Darnell said.

That sounded like an invitation to enter to me. Me and Maxi climbed the steps and skirted the boys on our way to the door. On the other side of the screen door a little girl held a headless doll. When I opened the door, she backed up, then ran off into the shadows of the house. The odor of mold, BO and dirty diapers assaulted my nose the second I stepped inside. Clothes, toys and empty food containers littered the floor. Some inane cartoon kept an infant in a playpen entertained. The baby held her diaper in one hand and scratched her butt with the other, then the child shoved the scratching finger up a nostril. I turned my head before I saw what she might pull out of the orifice.

I headed down the hall to my left assuming the bedrooms were that way. The first room I came to was wall-to-wall mattresses, dirty blankets and even dirtier clothes stacked up almost to the bottom of the window seal in places. Across the hall was another room with a closed door. I tapped lightly.

"Ms. Deadbeat?" I said.

Nothing.

"Hell," Maxi said as she turned the doorknob and walked in.

This room was cleaner than the rest of the house. The floor was clear other than a stack for clothes next to the bed. This mattress was on a bed frame. A black labeled whiskey bottle sat on the nightstand. Across the bed, Lizzy Deadbeat looked like a flaxen-haired ragdoll.

Maxi walked right over to the bed and tapped Lizzy on the shoulder.

"Hey, wake up!"

"Huh?" Lizzy jerked awake, pulled her hair out of her eyes and gave Maxi a bleary-eyed look. "How are you?" She slurred.

"I'm your fairy godmother and this..." she motioned to me, "...is your fairy godfather."

Lizzy snorted. "Yeah, right. What the fuck do you want?"

"You owe Shyster and Shyster five hundred and seventy-five dollars. We are here to collect," Maxi said.

Lizzy pushed herself up into a sitting position and sucked the snot out of her nose with a loud snort. What was it with snot in this family?

"Them women didn't even get me my child support from the IRS. I ain't payin' them. I gotta use that money to feed all these kids I bought."

"You did what?" Maxi asked.

"Nothin'," Lizzy said, looking away quickly. "Forget I said anything."

139

"Why don't you just pay us, and we'll get out of your hair," Maxi said. "Or we can stay here as long as it takes to *convince* you that it is in your *best* interest to pay up."

Lizzy gave Maxi a look that more than said Maxi should eat something foul smelling, such as the baby's diaper, and die. That wasn't a real good idea, but hey, it was no skin off my nose, so I didn't say nothin'.

In a split second, the small but lithe Maxi had Lizzy by the hair. She'd twisted the woman around and slammed her face first into the floor beside the bed. Maxi sat astride the stupid woman and pressed Lizzy's face into the floor.

"I tried to be nice, but noooo. There is no being nice with people like you, so now we will do it my way. Tell me where you keep your money. Jake here will take out the money you owe Shyster and Shyster while I consider how much hurt I can put on you," Maxi said.

That's my girl. I love it when she takes charge. Why, if she were two feet taller and twenty-five years older, I might fall in love, if she wouldn't kill me for doing it.

"There ain't no more money. I gave it to my bookie so he could double it for me, only that didn't work out so good." Lizzy tried to wiggle free, then she went to trying to buck Maxi off her back. Maxi used that as an excuse to dig her heels into Lizzy's sides and tighten her grip in the downed woman's hair.

"You dumb shit," Maxi said. "Women like you always have a stash. Where is it?"

"Ow! Ow! Ow! You dumb bitch! Get off me."

"You should talk nicer to the woman whose got your back." Maxi laughed and bounced up and down on Lizzy's back for emphasis. "Got your back, get it?"

"I got it," I said as a big smile spread across my face. "But I don't think Lizzy did. You might have to spell it out to her one broken rib at a time."

"No, don't do that!" Lizzy piped in between grunts and yelps.

"Then give us what we want," Maxi said.

"I don't have it to give, but I got something else."

"What's that?"

"Let me up first."

"I'll let you up," Maxi said, "but keep in mind that I can put you down again anytime I want."

Lizzy nodded and Maxi let her up. Lizzy wasn't going anywhere. I was between her and the door, not that Maxi needed my help with the skinny, little broad.

"Now what do you have to offer?" Maxi asked.

"I got me four little moneymakers. Them kids out there."

"Kids? What do you mean?" I asked. I hoped she wasn't suggesting what I thought she was. I didn't put up with much kiddy porn stuff.

"I mean IRS deductions and child support sources. I bought me four kids. Ms. Brigida got me a three-thousand-dollar refund off them kids. I give her one of the kids, and that will more than pay for my bill."

"You've got to be kidding," Maxi said.

Me? I was relieved she wasn't pimping out the kids. Some pervs would eat up a little boy like Darnell.

"No, no! Take your pick. The big 'uns are good for doing chores but the little 'uns bring more money on the open market, you know because you can claim them longer as dependents."

Maxi looked at me like she did

142

sometimes. It was the same look a semi-truck would give impending roadkill two seconds before flattening the animal into a misshapen pancake. That was the same look Maxi gave me the night she almost took my head off for suggesting she might possibly want to enjoy the company of a man sometime soon before her hormone-enraged tantrums ended up getting someone killed. She totally mistook what I was saying, honest.

"Maxi..." I warned. "...don't do it..."

"Do what?" Maxi asked.

"You know what."

"No, I don't."

"Yeah, you do. Don't do it, Maxi, there are kids in the other room."

"Why don't you take the kids for an ice cream?" Maxi said.

"What are you talking about?" Lizzy asked as she looked from one of us to the other.

"You don't want to know," I said.

"If it's about me, I damn well do want to know," Lizzy said.

"No, you don't," I argued. "It's really better if you don't see it coming."

Maxi pulled her sweatshirt off over her

head and tossed it to me. "Hold this. It's new. I don't want to get it bloody."

"Bloody!" Lizzy cried out as she started backpedaling toward the far wall. "No, freaking way! Take them all. I don't need no kids if it's gonna cost me my looks."

"Really?" I said, wondering what looks she was talking about. She was too skinny, too pale and her hair looked like she'd never learned how to use a conditioner after a shampoo. In fact, I questioned if she knew how to use the shampoo. A man of my stature and good upbringing notices these things.

Maxi advanced on Lizzy.

"Get this crazy bitch out of here," Lizzy said to me.

"Oh, I wouldn't call her that, if I were you," I said.

"Get her out and I'll throw in a baggy of weed and a BJ," Lizzy said.

"Lady, what makes you think I'd let you anywhere near my package?" I asked.

"Aw, come on, I ain't done no one no harm."

"Maxi," I said, "peace, love and harmony. Remember your anger management training."

"We all slip and fall, Jake," Maxi said.

"Not you, Maxi. You're as steadfast as they come."

"How about I just mostly hurt her?" Maxi slammed one miniature fist into a palm as she took another step toward Lizzy.

Lizzy hugged the wall. Her washed out looks blended into the dingy, once white wall except for the red-rimmed blue eyes. Glazed, the oversized orbs never left Maxi. I let Maxi take two more steps, enjoying her role as a tough before I called the show to a halt. As long as I had known Maxi, I had never seen her attack a downed opponent. I had no doubt she wouldn't hurt the pathetic woman, even if I didn't say something.

"Hey, Maxi, what do you say we take the kids, the weed and the rest of whiskey, then leave her here in this filth. I'll let you smack her around if she buys more kids next year. You know, that turn the other cheek thing?"

Maxi took a deep breath and let it out slowly. Her face melted from hardcore stone into an adolescent pout. She stomped a foot and stormed out the bedroom behind me, spouting, "You never let me have any fun!"

"I know, hun. I know," I said with a shrug toward the still cowering Lizzy.

Francine Zane

Chapter 18: Childhood Trauma

You can tell a lot about a kid by how quickly he will trade his freedom for a peanut butter cookie and a double fudge YooHoo. None of Lizzy's kids questioned us when we herded them toward the Caddy. The only things they took with them were the two clean diapers found next to the playpen and the headless doll that the little girl clutched to her chest like a life jacket.

We were in the car before a thought occurred to me.

"Hey, Maxi..."

"Yeah?"

"What are we doin' with them?"

Simultaneously, we twisted in our seats and looked at the kids in the backseat. Every single one had a runny nose and too many bruises to count.

"Darnell, who are your friends?" Maxi asked.

"That's Mikey. She's Chloe..." He pointed

at the girl with the headless doll. "...and the baby is Sugar."

"Where do you guys want to go?" Maxi asked.

The kids looked at one another and then shrugged.

"Don't you have families, moms, dads you want to go home to?"

Again the kids looked at each other.

"Why would we?" Darnell asked. "Nothing was any better with my mom than with Lizzy. She just smoked cigarettes all day and watched *The Jerry Springer Show*."

"What about grandparents?" I asked as I put the car into drive and pulled away from the curb. At the very least, we were getting out of the Forbidden Zone. The day was getting on, and a crowd of onlookers was gathering around the car. In this neighborhood, it was hard to tell when onlookers were apt to turn into an angry mob. One show of weakness, one batted eyelash at the wrong time and bam! The whole world became your enemy.

"Don't have any that I know of," Mikey said.

"What about the rest of you kids?" Maxi asked.

Hushed whispers ensued, then Darnell spoke up. "We decided we're going to be each other's family."

More whispers. A peek in the rearview mirror rewarded me with the little girl Chloe smiling a toothless smile at me.

"...and we want you to be family too," Darnell announced.

Me and Maxi looked at each other in bewilderment. No one had ever wanted to be family with us before. My heart melted down to about half its normal size, and I saw tears well in my tough Maxi's eyes, partly because she knew what I knew. We weren't the parentin' types. If these kids stayed with us, they'd all grow up mean, ugly and probably in jail before they learned how to kiss the opposite sex. No, sweet as these kids might be, we wouldn't be raisin' 'em.

"Do you have any aunts or uncles," Maxi said, her voice as soft and loving as I'd ever heard it.

"No!" came the united response from the back seat.

"Sure you do! I'm Aunt Maxi and this is your Uncle Jake. Anyone messes with you from now on, and they gotta take us on. Now who is up for a YooHoo?"

149

"What's a YooHoo?" Chloe asked in a birdlike voice.

"You don't know what a YooHoo is?" I asked. "Why a YooHoo is the most rootin-tootin best chocolate soda in the whole world! You ain't lived if you haven't had a YooHoo."

We crossed out of the Forbidden Zone and found a convenience store that sold YooHoo. It took us about three stops, but by now, the kids wouldn't settle for anything less than a chocolate soda.

Afterward, we took them to a park with a working fountain. While the kids cleaned up in the fountain, Maxi and I came up with a plan. If we took them to the cops, they might end up back with parents who would just sell them again. That was no good. So we were left with only one logical option.

Maxi made a phone call while I loaded the kids back into the car. I cringed as their wet little bodies squeaked along the car's fine leather seats, but you couldn't have paid me to say nothin'. These were part my kids now and could do no wrong.

We drove over to Shyster and Shyster. Maxi had called ahead and made sure Ms. Brigida was there. Ms. Brigida, now she was one fine woman. Classy, smart and just enough clumsy to be cute. One day some man would be real lucky if she fell into his arms. And the woman had a big heart only she didn't know it yet. She was about to learn.

We let ourselves in the front office. The place was dead this time of the year. No customers. No workers but Ms. Shyster and Ms. Brigida. I led the kids over to the waiting room chairs.

"Now you kids sit here and be real still. We gotta talk to Ms. Brigida," I said.

"Are you going to sell us to her?" Chloe asked, her lower lip quivering.

"No, hun. I'd never sell you, but I do gotta find a good place for you to call home. Ms. Brigida here, now she is one smart woman. She'll help us." I said.

"Can't we stay with you and Maxi?" Darnell asked.

"No, me and Maxi aren't the parenting type. We are the aunt and uncle type. You get me?"

Slowly, the kids nodded. They weren't happy about it. Here we had pulled them out of one bad situation, and now they were doomed to go somewhere else new and scary.

I followed Maxi into Ms. Brigida's office with one last look back at the kids. I put my finger to my lip as a reminder to keep it quiet while we talked.

"How goes it Maxi...Jake?" Ms. Brigida asked.

She looked awfully cute sitting there in faded jeans and an oversized t-shirt. Her hair was tousled, and she wore pink nail polish on her toes and fingers.

"All done with the collections work I gave you? How much did you recoup?"

I looked at Maxi. She looked at me. Neither one of us knew how to start this conversation, but I was the man, so I took the lead.

"No, ma'am. Not exactly."

"What do you mean?" Ms. Brigida asked.

"Well, we decided to hit up Lizzy Deadbeat first, seeing as she lives out in the Forbidden Zone, and it's safer to traverse out there when people are still passed out."

"And?"

"And she didn't have the money. What she did have was a bag of weed, a half bottle of whiskey and four kids..."

Ms. Brigida turned pale. She held up a

hand to stop me.

"Don't tell me. Please don't tell me she gave you a child as payment."

"Oh no, ma'am. That's what she wanted to do, but me and Maxi said no."

Maxi and I nodded in unison. Ms. Brigida looked relieved.

"Thank goodness! That woman trades kids the way the Indians traded the white man furs and beads for cloth and flour. And I have no idea what I would do with a kid running around here breaking things and wiping infant cooties all over the place. Why, one of my crystal figurines burst the last time those kids were here just from being in the proximity."

"Here's the weed." I handed her the bag of marijuana. "You don't want the whiskey. Cheap stuff. Tastes like kerosene mixed with sauerkraut. Bad stuff."

Ms. Brigida said, "I don't smoke weed, but I have a feeling you are going to tell me something that will make me want to start." She took the baggy and slipped it into the top drawer of her desk. "Or I guess I could sell it to someone with glaucoma."

"Sure you can," I said. Stalling for all I was worth. "That's a good idea. Isn't it a good idea, Maxi." I looked to my sidekick for encouragement. She gave none. She didn't even look in my direction.

Ever one for subtle conversation, Maxi said, "We took all four of those kids she bought in exchange for the money she owed you. They're out there." She hooked a thumb toward the reception area.

"You did what!" Ms. Brigida said as she jumped up and made a dash for the door.

She slammed the door open so hard, a couple of her little glass figurines jumped off the shelf and committed suicide. Lolla Brigida stopped as if caught in a force field and made an exaggerated about-face. The sound that came out of her throat was a cross between a cry and a whimper. She reached out toward the shelf of figurines and then the floor, then back toward the children who were still sitting where we left them in the reception area.

I made a mental note to buy Ms. Brigida two glass figurines per child and leave them with a note of apology from the kids. Course it wasn't the kids' fault the little glass do-hickies were broken, but I had a feeling Ms. Brigida wouldn't see it that way. Besides, glass do-hickies were cheap. I knew a guy over on Witchit Street who would sell me a dozen for a couple of bucks.

"I...I...who...when...parents???" Ms. Brigida said.

I grabbed her desk chair and rolled it behind her until the seat touched the back of her legs, then eased her down into it.

"It's alright, Ms. Brigida. We already asked the kids if they wanted to go home. They voted to stay together. Ain't that great? You got a full-fledged family all ready to go."

"Me?" Ms. Brigida asked staring from me to Maxi.

I put my hands on my knees and leaned in close to Ms. Brigida. "Yeah, you can't leave them innocent kids with the likes of us, can you?"

"No, I guess not," she whispered. "But me!" She rose to her feet and looked around as if she had just awakened on a foreign planet.

Aw, why did she have to agree so quickly? She could have at least argued that we were parent material, at least a little bit to spare our feelings. Here I was giving her the benefit of the doubt, and according to Lizzy, Ms. Brigida knew all about the kids bein' sold.

155

"You have an ethical obligation to protect these kids from a woman like that Deadbeat chick," Maxi said.

"Uh huh," the catatonic Ms. Brigida mumbled.

"Kids, this is Ms. Brigida. She's gonna take care of you now. Come over here and introduce yourself," Maxi motioned them forward. "Mikey, you first..."

"I'm Mikey. I'm ten. I like cars."

Darnell stepped forwards. "I'm Darnell. I want to stay with Maxi and Jake."

"Now, Darnell, we discussed this," I said.

Darnell nodded. "Yeah, but I don't have to like it."

Chloe took a step back and hid behind Darnell. "Chloe."

"How old are you Chloe?" Ms. Brigida managed.

"I don't know."

"What happened to your doll?"

"Nothin'."

"It has no head," Ms. Brigida observed.

"She never had a head."

Baby Sugar dropped to all fours and approached Ms. Brigida like an infant freight train. Ms. Brigida cringed and pulled her legs up beneath her. She placed a death grip on my hand.

"It's ok," I said. "Sugar's just a baby. She wants to say hi."

Ms. Brigida's grip loosened as Sugar stopped and used Ms. Brigida's chair to pull herself up into a standing position. Happy with her accomplishment, Sugar smiled and bounced.

"I don't know nothin' 'bout raisin' no babies," Ms. Brigida paraphrased Prissy from *Gone with the Wind*.

That was a good sign. If she had enough wits about her to quote old movies, she must be coming around. She'd be alright. She was a smart woman. She'd figure this out.

"I tell you what, you stay here and get acquainted with the kids. Me and Maxi will go do some shoppin' for ya."

"Don't forget the YooHoo...and diapers. Lots of diapers," Darnell suggested. "Sug always needs her diaper changed."

As if on cue, the small wonder bounced a wet squirt from her diaper region that was accompanied by a man-sized stink.

I think Ms. Brigida passed out.

Francine Zane

Chapter 19: The Holy Trinity

"I am not taking these kids home with me!" I stated with all the emphasis I had left in me after changing Sugar's diaper twice in ten minutes. How could one little body have so much poop? Okay, granted, if a body that small could hold that much poop, then so much poop would not likely have to escape, but still...what do you feed a kid to create so much nuclear waste byproduct?

"Well, I can't take them. I live in an adult's only condo. Even my cat had to be an adult before they would let me move her in. Poor thing had to live in a kitten cubby at the vet for the first year of her life," Janet said.

"Why didn't you just adopt an adult cat then?"

"Kittens are so much cuter, don't you think?"

I had to admit they were, but...never mind. We were way off topic here.

"The kids! Janet focus. What are we doing with the kids?"

"They're your kids, not mine. I didn't know anything about buying kids for tax credits. I would have called the authorities the minute I found out."

"Oh, we could turn them over to the authorities. Why didn't I think of that?"

Janet said, "You would really do that to those kids now? They've been through so much already, and now you want to put them in foster care? That's kind of harsh, don't you think?"

"But you said..."

"Never mind what I said. Look at them..."

The boys had taken over Andrew's old cube and were playing video games on the computer. Chloe and Sugar had conked out in the middle of the floor for a midday nap. I'd laid down a couple of trash bags first, in the event Sugar launched a repeat attack of the leaking diaper monster, then covered the girls with an old jacket sized to fit a small buffalo that I dug out of the lost and found. I had considered putting them down in one of the recliners with the foot raised but figured the closer they were to the floor, the better the odds they wouldn't fall. After the day these kids had lived, they didn't need to add bumps and even more bruises to the mix.

Yeah, foster care would be adding insult to injury. Besides, the authorities would likely try to return them to their parents who might just turn around and sell them for more cigarettes, a pack of gum or a shot of Jack Daniels again. What these kids needed was some stability. Well, and maybe a bath...or two. Clean clothes might help as well, an education. Possibly a doll with an actual head on it. Who was I kidding? What they really needed were parents. Good parents. The kind that knew how to take care of them, what to feed them to prevent poop monsters and who knew good bedtime stories by heart, not just because they were good at Googling the information up. At the very least, they needed parents who weren't afraid of them.

Yes, I was afraid. Really, really afraid not only of what they might do, like destroy my entire life but also of what I might do to screw their young lives up even worse than they already were.

"What about Henry and Henrietta?

Couldn't they…"

Janet interrupted me, "No. They are in Florida now, remember, not to mention we decided they are freaking crazy. Crazy doesn't make for stable parenting."

"Amen to that, sista'." I knew that one from personal experience.

And then it happened. A stranger walked into the store sporting a tailored black suit, matching umbrella and the ugliest shoes on earth. On top of her meticulously styled golden curls, she wore a halo—I kid you not. A real honest to goodness halo that emitted a heavenly glow. The voices of a million angels sang the sweetest song I'd ever heard—*Love Is Like a Butterfly*, originally performed by Dolly Parton.

The song ended and the woman spoke, "Hello, ladies. Is this the business of Shyster and Shyster? I'm looking for the masterminds of the Church of Perpetual Profits."

"We are," I said.

"My name is Tracillia Numbchucks. I understand you are in need of a bible ghostwriter."

I looked at Janet, who slapped a hand across her face. "Oh, God, I forgot. I hired a ghostwriter for the bible."

"Please do not use the Lord's name in vain," Tracillia said. "Not in my presences and preferably not ever!"

"Yes, ma'am." Janet and I said in unison.

"I've come to interview you before I start writing. Shall we begin?" And then she spotted the children. "Oh my! What lovely children. Are they yours?" She looked from one partner to the other.

"Well, sort of," I said.

"Well, are they or are they not? You either have children or you do not. Come, come, you should know the answer to this one."

"It's a long story, but in general they were traded to us to pay off a debt," I said.

"That must have been some debt."

"No, not really, but our debt collectors are really good at what they do."

Tracillia measured our worth with serious eyes then said, "What do you intend to do with these children?"

"We were just discussing that. Do you have any suggestions?" I asked.

"Are they well behaved?" Tracillia asked.

"Probably not. They're kids."

"Do they say their prayers before eating?"

"Nope, at least not before eating candy bars and potato chips, which is all we've fed them so far."

"Do they brush their teeth before bed?"

"I've not seen a single toothbrush since they got here."

"And you? Do you know anything about parenting?"

"I know that I'm totally unqualified to even own a pet, does that count?" I said.

"And what about you?" Tracillia asked Janet.

"I have a cat but my cat has a nanny, so..."

Tracillia nodded. "I see."

"Well then," Tracillia said as she straightened her halo, "I have no choice. I will take the children. Feed them, care for them, educate them and prepare their souls for eternal salvation. You..." she pointed at Janet and me, "...will do three things."

"Yes?"

"You own the school turned church building, yes?"

We nodded.

"You will convert a block of six rooms

into an orphanage. I will also need another room as a private chapel. You will pay me for my ghostwriting duties by allowing me to incorporate the Sisterhood of the Divine Power into your church. I will act as Mother Superior and provide my own habits. The church will pay all of our expenses and provide for the children's higher education. Is that clear?"

"Yes, ma'am," I said. Relief coursed through my body.

"And now I must tell my husband I am leaving him for a better man. Please have the children ready for me in exactly one hour." Tracillia turned on her grotesquely clad heels and headed for the door.

And that, my dear friends, is how the Church of Perpetual Profits gained but an orphanage and a nunnery, both of which cost money to operate, and neither of which make money.

"Janet?"

"Yes?"

"We're never going to show a profit again, are we?"

"Not likely, no."

Things just kept getting better and better.

Francine Zane

Chapter 20: Maxi Climbs the Hightower

"Maxi, we gotta do better with this next collection. We owe Ms. Brigida big time for all she's doing for those kids."

"Jake, I know how to act in polite society, but you, you I'm not so sure about."

"What do you mean?" I asked.

"When was the last time you were in polite society?"

"The last time you were, I suspect."

Of course, I wasn't really sure what constituted polite society. I considered Ms. Shyster and Ms. Brigida polite society, but that was different than what Maxi was talking about. What she was really talking about was Tiffany Hightower society, which was more about dealing with the rich than with the polite. Sometimes, they were the same thing but sometimes not. I suspected Mrs. Hightower, bein' as she was great-granddaughter of one of the wealthiest men in the Midwest, could be both polite and "unpolite," just depended on who she faced. Facing someone like Maxi and I imagined Mrs. Hightower would get a lot of "unpolite" practice.

The Hightower estate was located as far from the Forbidden Zone as an estate could get and still share the same solar system, but the real distance between the estate and the Forbidden Zone had nothin' to do with distance. It had a lot to do with the attitude of the inhabitants. The people of the Forbidden Zone either felt the world owed them or that the world had crapped on them during a universal colonoscopy cleansing. Mrs. Hightower and her neighbors felt they owed no one because only the worthy would ever aspire to greatness. Never mind how many of these wealthy elitists inherited their wealth, often from criminals or the ethically challenged who had never been successfully prosecuted. Either way, their money was a gift from the gods not from their own hard work.

Me, I work for my money. I have since I was a kid. I like earning what I got. In a way, I feel as sorry for the Hightowers in the world as I do the Forbidden Zone inhabitants. They might live better than me. They might drive nicer cars and take more vacations, but they don't know the satisfaction of earning what they spend. It's kind of like Halloween for kids. After the initial excitement of dressin' up, trick or treating and coming home with your weight in candy wears off, the candy just don't taste as good. It's all empty calories with no substance.

Mrs. Hightower expected us at two. We arrived at the outer gate at ten minutes till. Five minutes later, we arrived at the inner gate. Ten minutes later, we pulled up in the circle drive and was greeted by an old codger in a black suit. His shoes were admirably shined to a high sheen. I made a mental note to ask him how he got such a good shine. I'm always lookin' for good tips to a high shine.

The codger showed us into a room with lots of books and leather, and these weren't cheap paperbacks either. These books had leather spines and gold lettering in many cases. I took a deep breath and smelled the intoxicating mixture of wood, leather, cigar smoke and old money. Good. It's easier to collect money from people who have it than those who don't.

I followed the scent of cigar smoke to the elderly woman sitting in a wingback chair. The woman wore an open burgundy velvet housecoat that looked like it belonged to a man from another century. Beneath the housecoat, she wore white flannel pajamas covered with petite pink flowers. Her shoes were pink fluffy slippers.

I liked the old codger better.

"Good afternoon," the woman said before taking a pull on the cigar and blowing out a stream of gray and white smoke. "It's about time we met, Jake."

I was surprised she knew my name.

"You must be Tiffany Hightower," I said.

"Yes, and this..." Tiffany Hightower looked Maxi up and down, then dismissed her. "...little person must be Maxine Precious. I had heard she was on the short side."

I heard Maxi curse under her breath, and I put a hand on her arm, ready to hold her back if necessary. Women like Mrs. Hightower had the resources to put a real hurt on someone like Maxi, if provoked.

"Yeah, it is," I said, somewhat confused as to how she knew our names.

"Why don't you send your...little friend...to the kitchen. Chef always has some snacks available. We need to talk."

"Maxi goes where I go," I said. "But, yeah, we need to talk. The ladies at Shyster and Shyster sent us."

"And it is about time, too. I was beginning to wonder how much of a bill they would let me build up before they sent you to collect." She motioned to the leather couch across a glossy coffee table from her. "Please sit."

We sat across from the old woman and watched as she puffed on the cigar again.

"This is an awful habit, isn't it?" Mrs. Hightower said.

We neither agreed nor disagreed. Why would we? Everyone has bad habits. This appeared to be hers.

"I picked it up after my brother died. My grandfather, father and brother all smoked. I miss the odor, I guess." Softly she added, "I miss them."

"What's all this have to do with the money you owe Shyster and Shyster?" Maxi asked.

The look Mrs. Hightower gave Maxi could have killed a weaker woman. "It doesn't, Ms. Maxwell. Not one little bit other than it got Jake here in front of me."

The more the woman talked, the more confused I became.

"Now, if you don't mind, I would like you both to remain quiet and listen until I'm done telling my story. Afterward, I will write Ms. Shyster and Ms. Brigida a check that will pay my outstanding bill plus enough to cover the next twelve months. Do we have an agreement?"

Me and Maxi looked at one another, then back at the old woman. We nodded in unison. This job was gonna be easier than we thought.

"Jake, you are what? About fifty-five? Fifty-six?" Mrs. Hightower asked.

"Fifty-seven."

"And your mother never married your father, is that correct?"

"Yeah, I'm a bastard. What of it?" I wanted to ask what my paternity had to do with her, but one thing livin' as long as I have has taught me. Sometimes you learn more by listening than by talkin'.

Mrs. Hightower nodded, her eyes focused on something far away. "Yes, I guess that is about right. I was a young woman then. Barely a woman really. Seventeen. My father and my brother were both alive then. We were happy together, or at least I thought so until that night.

She looked back at me then, her eyes bright, alive. "It was after Thanksgiving and before Christmas. I remember the staff had already decorated these rooms for the holiday. My father and William, my brother, were in this room, smoking cigars and reading newspapers when I entered. Back then, we all read at least two newspapers a day, unlike now. Now, you turn on the TV or a computer if you want to stay current.

"Something in the paper caught my father's attention. He folded the paper open to the article and passed it to William. Then next thing I knew, Father sent me to my room.

"It wasn't until much later that I found out what happened. It wasn't the story in the paper that had upset my father. It was an accompanying picture. The picture showed William holding a baby and standing next to him was a woman and two other children. You see, my dear brother played the high society playboy within our circle and family man for your mother and you. A double life, because he knew Father would never accept William's relationship with...with...that woman—your mother. She didn't have the upbringing or the financial connections that Father had expected from a marriage.

"William began spending more time away, I presume with you and less with us, which was probably a good thing because Father and William fought a lot. Eventually, the fights grew more volatile. I remember hearing things breaking from my room. I remember William demanding his rights as a man and Father swearing like I'd never heard him swear before. And then one day, the fight just stopped in mid-sentence. Father had a stroke and was bedridden, and I was left alone to deal with him and all the other responsibilities of running this place. You see, William had stormed out of the house the night of the stroke before realizing how ill Father really was.

"I thought William had run off to be with you and your mother. I grew to hate you all for taking him away from me when I needed him the most, then I learned he deserted you, too. I felt guilty as if I had something to do with a little boy not having a father to grow up with and guide him. So, I depended on a family friend to make sure your mother was taken care of and that you would always have a job. For a long time, I had no idea the friend was not a completely honest man or that your jobs were less than legitimate. By the time I did, you had already chosen another path for yourself as a collector, so I left you alone to be the man you chose to be."

"What about my father, I mean William? What happened to him?" I asked, my head still wrapping around what she was saying.

"I don't really know. Oh, I had people search for him off and on over the years, but he just walked out the door and vanished."

"Why are you telling me this now?" I asked.

"Father died and I married Mr. Hightower, who was a good man but not particularly affectionate. We never had children, so when he died, I was all alone again. For a while, alone is not so bad. I can do what I want. Go where I want. But the older I get, the more I miss what I once had. I miss family. I miss having people in my life that I actually love instead of just tolerate."

She stubbed out the cigar butt. "And I

miss the smell of aftershave, cigars and good leather."

"So, you are telling me you are my aunt?" I asked.

"Yes, Jake. I am your aunt, and as far as my detectives have been able to determine, we are the only family we have left."

I thought about all the years I had wondered why my dad had disappeared. I remembered the smell of cigars on his coat when he hugged me. I remembered how sad mom was when he left. I'm fifty-seven years old. I know I can't live in the past, but I also know I would never willingly give up those memories.

I knew I should be mad or sad or something over the news Mrs. Hightower had just imparted to me, but honestly, I didn't feel much different. I loved my dad for the time he spent with me. As far as I can remember, all that time was good time. He never made me feel like a second-class citizen. Of course, the time we had together was short, but there were a lot of kids whose parents had married who had later found themselves in a one parent home. And I don't remember my mom saying anything bad about Dad either. In fact, one of the last conversations I had with Mom, she told me that she still missed him. That was a long time to miss someone.

Now here was another person who missed him. This stranger with so much money and yet was so lonely. Maybe I'd feel different later after I thought about it more, but right then, I just felt sorry for her. As far as I saw it, I got the best part of my dad. She got the leftovers.

True to her word, Mrs. Hightower wrote out a big check to Shyster and Shyster. She offered me another check. I told her to keep it. At least for now. Before she called in the old codger, who I now know is named Grievous, to see us out, she made me promise to visit again, and I will. I'd like to know more about my dad and my history. Besides, the old lady isn't so bad. She's gotta have spunk to have live so long and through so much loss.

Francine Zane

Chapter 21: Blessed Be Thy Return

"Lolla, do you have a minute?" Janet asked from my open office door.

"Sure, what is up?"

"How do you feel about baptism?"

I thought about the question a moment, considering all the possible implications. Once you start a church as a tax shelter and hire a married nun to write a bible, pretty much every question could mean more than one thing. Ask a question like how do you feel about baptism and my mind starts coming up with a thousand possible scenarios. The first of which is whether I personally have been baptized or would care to be baptized. I decided to go with a non-answer.

"It depends."

"On?"

"Why are you asking? No, I don't want to be baptized into the Church of Perpetual

Profits, but yes, I'm good to go if someone else wants baptized. No, I don't think we need to invest in a dunking tank for the job, but yes, if you want to open a new revenue stream by creating holy water for baptisms, vampire slaying and exorcisms, I'm open to the possibility, once we get a permanent Guide. I don't think this Father Arnold that we borrowed from the Temple of Holy Rollers is the man for the job. Even he fell asleep during his last sermon."

Janet made herself comfortable on my couch. "I'm working on that. The Tabernacle of Misfit Toys is sending over a Church Jester for next week's sermon. I hear he got nines across the board during his last Blessed Words pray off. He would have gotten tens, but when he lapsed into speaking in tongues, no one got his jokes."

"I suppose we could ask Mother Superior Tracillia to step in."

Janet said, "Are you asking her because I'm not. I'm scared of her."

"Now that you mention it, so am I, especially since she started carrying around that ruler. I cringe every time she slaps it against the side of her habit."

Janet nodded. "I saw her use it on one of

the carpenters who was renovating her private chapel. She can weld that ruler faster than a quick-draw gunslinger. The guy acted like his hand would fall off after she hit him, too."

"Why did she hit him?"

"He was singing along with his iPod while installing the crucifix and the altar."

"That's all?" I asked.

"Well, he was singing *Black Sabbath.*"

"Ah, that would do it." I nodded. "Are we in for a lawsuit over this?"

"No. Apparently his mother goes to the same gynecologist as Mother Tracillia. Tracillia called his mother, and she made him do the rest of the work for free in retribution."

I shuddered at the thought of a nun even having the equipment necessary to visit a gynecologist and quickly pushed the image out of my mind. "Woot! The Lord does work in mysterious ways."

"Not so fast with spending our savings, Lolla."

"Um...doesn't spending defeat the concept of saving?" I asked.

"Tell Mother Superior that."

"Oh no. Now what?"

"She decided that since we saved so much money on the remodeling, we have the money to open a gravy kitchen," Janet said.

"You mean a soup kitchen? For feeding the homeless?"

Janet thought about it a second. "No, I'm pretty sure I got it right. She wants a gravy kitchen because gravy is a comfort food, and homeless people need comfort more than anyone else she knows."

Always thinking, I said, "Maybe we can give away the gravy and make the money in upcharges, such as biscuits and sausages."

"Right, because the homeless have so much spare change since they don't pay rent and utilities." Janet's sarcasm was showing.

"Exactly! I hear a good hobo can make as much standing on a street corner begging each day as I made working as a dishwasher at Denny's while I was in college, and I just bet the hobo doesn't leave the city owing six-digit student loan bills."

"Lolla! You can't make fun of the homeless. It isn't done."

"Who is making fun of them? I envy their ability to keep costs down. The average hobo is doing far better than we are. At the rate we are going, we'll be the first ones standing in the gravy line!"

"Speak for yourself. Buff usually has dinner ready for me before I get home. He cooks enough to feed a family of four. I've got a freezer filled with leftovers. I'm good for at least six months of losses."

"I'll tell your mortgage holder that. I'm sure he will be comforted. Now, back to the original question. What about baptism are you questioning?"

"Do you remember Fire Marshal Puff N. Stuff?"

"The puffy white guy who sits in the front row shelling peanuts and popping them in his mouth between amens?"

"That's the guy. Well, he came in to see me last week. He's undergone an IRS audit every year since 1967. He is feeling a bit targeted for his political affiliation."

"What is his political affiliation?" I asked.

"He's a member of the Teacup Party."

"You mean the Tea Party?" Janet was an angel but not very savvy sometimes. I loved her anyway.

"No. I mean the Teacup Party. It's a Rainbow Party offshoot. The Teacup Party is a group of political activists."

"What makes them special?"

"Well, they are all over fifty, wealthy businessmen who just happen to like to dress in women's clothing and sing *I Am Woman*."

"The old Helen Reddy song?"

"That's the one."

"Okay...that is a little odd but no reason for targeting."

"Well, strictly according to the fire marshal, it is if you won't let certain people who live in white houses play with you."

"White houses? A lot of people live in white—"

"But this white house resident also has the power to launch an apocalyptic missile attack on practically the whole world with the push of a big red Easy button."

I nodded. "Oh, that resident...really? No way. Really?"

Janet held up a hand to hold me off. "I'm only repeating what I was told."

"And he thinks the IRS tracks political affiliation?"

"Well, yeah, right next to his shoe size, how often he brushes his teeth and the number of times he goes potty each day."

"Hey! That would explain why the IRS's resources are stretched so thin."

"Exactly!"

"So what does Fire Marshal Stuff want us to do about it?"

"He has a three-pronged plan. First prong, he has had six accountants do his taxes this year. The goal was to compare the balance due on each return and file the return that the most accountants agreed was for the correct amount. The problem was all six returns ended up with three different balances due."

"Figures." Hard to be surprised at pretty much anything lately.

"Prong two, he wants to come to us for a tie breaker return, and prong three is to have the return blessed by the Church. In exchange for our part in the plan, he will commit to an annual tithing that would just about pay for the cost of the gravy kitchen.

"However, there is a catch. If he is audited after the blessing, we are responsible for dealing with the IRS for free."

"Yikes!" Free wasn't in my vocabulary. Free didn't pay the student loan payments or the mortgage. Free definitely didn't fatten the Me account for my absolutely must have—"

"Exactly, but if we can convince enough of the congregation to follow suit, odds are we can make money."

I nodded even as I came up with one really killer reason it couldn't work. "Presuming everyone files an honest return. We completed an entire tax season on a platform of filing mostly correct returns and fully expecting the IRS to audit a percentage of our returns."

"True. We would must include a carefully worded out clause. Not even God can be held responsible for the sins of the guilty."

And boy were we guilty. In less than a year, we had gone from borderline crooks to out and out sinners who use religion as the primary focus to our business plan. We have made a mockery of our profession and our faith. We were going to hell. I mean real hell, the kind of hell where fire and brimstone are the highlights.

I pictured hell as an unending deluge of bad poetry, poor hygiene and rock beds, which I would fall out of into the bottomless fiery pit on a daily basis, only to be fished out with a tuna hook to do it all over again.

Mrs. Hightower would probably be there, just to not listen to me in our usual one-sided conversations, and mother and grandmother would pop in to see if I am pregnant yet at least once a year.

Hot men in loincloths would always be right out of reach, and my student loan payments would follow me into Hades. The devil himself would laugh and shake my hand for being an even bigger numb nuts than he was when it comes to getting the attention of the Holy Father.

Maybe that was the problem. Maybe all of this had more to do with me seeking the attention of the father I never had. If I couldn't have the love of a human father, maybe some time over the last year, I'd decided to gain the attention of my heavenly father. Like so many purportedly bad kids, though, the only way I could subconsciously come up with to gain his attention was by doing something so outrageous that he would have no choice but to pay attention. How warped was that?

Why Janet was going along on this ride with me was beyond me. The woman was so serious and conscientious. She had class and seemed to really care about our clients, at least a lot more than I did. Had Jake and Maxi not shamed me into it, I would likely have given those bought and sold kids a twenty and sent them on their way. Well, maybe not, but I would never have considered opening an orphanage, and I definitely would not have taken them home with me, probably. But then again, when that baby pulled herself up next to me and laughed, for that one split second and then again when the girl Chloe told me her doll never had a head, for those two seconds I could almost see myself with children. I almost believed I could do a better job than their parents, or my own. But then Mother Superior had arrived and taken the situation out of my hands. At the time, I thought of it as a miracle, but now I wonder. I wonder if she arrived not as a miracle but as punishment. My one opportunity to become a parent perhaps forever now gone.

"Let's do it," I said. "Let's go balls to the wall. Baptisms, exorcisms, blessings, curses, tithing, everything. Mother Superior can even have her gravy kitchen."

"Okay then," Janet got to her feet. "I'd better have a few things added to the bible."

Chapter 22: Let There Be a Guide

"You still looking for a Guide?" Maxi asked, her feet swinging back and forth beneath my guest chair.

"We are," I said, just a little confused at what was going on here.

Maxi had entered my office a couple of minutes ago. Her now black pigtails were curly ringlets that stood out from her scalp like little pompoms. She wore a black and white striped shirt beneath a leather boyfriend jacket. She had layered a black skater skirt over black stockings. Black fingerless gloves accentuated creamy hands tipped with burgundy nail polish. The nail polish matched the patent leather Mary Janes. This was as close to conservative as I had ever seen the woman.

"I'd like to apply."

I almost spit out the mouthful of Starbucks non-fat, no foam, decaffeinated, sugar-free excuse for a beverage I had mistakenly taken. Instead, I gulped it down and felt it scorch a trail down to my suddenly painful ulcer.

"I'm sorry. What did you say?" I asked.

"I've got a master's degree in philosophy with a bachelor's in public speaking. I speak six languages, including Latin, and I work cheap. What do you have to lose?" Maxi asked. Her expression never changed from the stone cold ball buster I had always thought her to be.

"Maxi, are you sure you want to be a Guide? It's like a priest or pastor, you know. You'd need to prepare sermons and, you know, make people feel welcomed and, you know, loved." I couldn't picture Maxi making anyone feel loved.

"I know what a religious leader does," Maxi said. "I'm not stupid. And, I can be..." She gulped. "...friendly. I've just never chosen to be before now...friendly that is."

"Why now?"

"When I had Jake, I didn't need anyone else. He had my back. Now he's spending all his time with old lady Hightower learning about his heritage or some such. I got no one again, and I don't like it. So, I figured if

I'm a Guide, I can make enough friends and influence enough lives never to be alone again. Besides, I'm getting too old for the collections business. Kicking the sh—, sorry, subduing lowlifes takes a lot out of a person. And, I went to the trouble of buying these degrees from one of the best online schools in the nation. I figure I might as well use them."

"You bought them?" I asked, so not impressed.

"Yeah, didn't you?"

She was right. Sure I put in the work, but if I hadn't paid the fees, there was no way I would have received a degree.

"I suppose you're right, but really? You think Guide is your calling?"

"As much as shyster is yours," Maxi said with a huge grin. She leaned forward in her seat and rested her hands on her knees. She looked me in the eyes with all the solemnity of priest listening to a confession.

"I'll tell you what. You give me one month. That's four services to work out all the kinks. If attendance goes up, I get the job. If it goes down or stagnates, I'll go back to collections. If you give me the job, I take ten percent of the profits, not counting the orphanage, nunnery or the gravy kitchen. Those belong to Mother Superior. I won't step on her toes."

"Those endeavors are all money pits. The church tithes and collections have to pay for them as well as salaries, utilities, the mortgage...I'd like to get paid, too, eventually..."

Maxi nodded. "Okay, I see your point. I'll drop my fee down to eight percent during the first year. I get a one percent increase each of the next three years that the church increases profits. Oh! And I want three rooms of the school for my private quarters."

"Do we have to pay for the renovations?" I asked.

"Not at all! I'll pay for my own rooms, but I want to be ensured total privacy."

Alarm bells went off in my head. What if this was the female equivalent of a Catholic priest pimping out a stable of altar boys to all his brethren?

"Um...counteroffer...you can maintain total privacy provided the Church does not receive a single complaint questioning the legality of what happens in those rooms. I can't have a perv bringing the Church down..." I put up a hand, palm out. "...not saying you are a perv, but holy men have a reputation you'll have to live down."

Maxi considered my offer, then got to her feet and put out her hand. "Done!"

"Done!"

"Oh wait!" Maxi took back her hand without shaking. "Two more points...I want the Church to pay for my costuming. I'll pay for my own during the trial period, but afterward, I will need a wardrobe and makeup specialist and a costuming budget. Let's say one percent of the take? Any costs over that come out of my share of the profits. Second, I want to be called Precious Heart."

With that request, her normal tough exterior melted. Maxi looked as innocent and young as her attire attested. I had always thought of Maxi as in her late thirties or early forties—something closer to her cohort Jake's age. But right then, I could never have guessed.

"Guide Precious Heart, that has a ring to it," I said and nodded. "Alright, Guide Heart..."

"Guide Precious Heart," Maxi corrected.

"Guide Precious Heart, then I have one last condition. Before each sermon, you must present your sermon to us for approval. We can't afford promises that may implicate us in something illegal like tax fraud, evasion, money laundering or identity theft. We are already pushing the limits with developing a religion around financial security rather than some mystical deity."

"Does the sermon have to be word for word?"

I wanted to say yes, but from my brief and oh so unsuccessful experience with the media, I knew how hard it was to stick strictly to a script, and I couldn't imagine how much tougher it must be with a live audience. With a live audience, anything could happen, kind of like the break dancer during the first service.

"How about we agree that you will stick to the spirit of the written sermon and see how it goes?"

"I know. What if you give me a signal when you think I am straying too far from the approve script?"

"What did you have in mind?"

"Well, an ear tug worked for Carol Burnett," Maxi suggested.

"Let's shake on it." And this time, when I put out my hand, Maxi didn't pull back.

Yea, me! We had a new head for this turkey of an enterprise we had created. Maybe now the Church would stop flopping around pointlessly. In all the time I had known her, Maxi had maintained her sanity even during insane times. She had a unique look, too. And she smelled good, darn it, like cinnamon bread. Gotta love that.

Francine Zane

Chapter 23: Guide Precious Heart

Clothes never meant a lot to me. I have three gray suits, two navy suits, three brown suits and a half dozen blouses that I can mix and match to my heart's content. I own four pairs of leather work shoes. My leisure time wardrobe is even more limited. Maybe that is why it didn't occur to me to retain costume approval for Precious Heart. Now it was too late. The auditorium was almost full. If we didn't send someone out on stage soon, we would lose a lucrative opportunity to share fellowship with like minds. Do you like how I nicely I managed to turn my thoughts from money to something more churchy?

If only Janet was as proud of me as I was of myself. Ever since I hired Guide Precious Heart, all she has said is, "Seriously?" then cross her arms under her bosom and shake her head. It is really hard to hold a conversation within those limitations. I could only hope and pray Precious didn't let me down.

Precious Heart had presented her sermon and waited patiently for me to approve it. All Janet would say was, "Seriously?" and walk off. I chose to take that as an approval, so who could I blame now for the sight before me? Surely not Janet—or Precious. I never asked what the costuming thing was all about. I thought she was referring to robes and a crucifix, kind of like she referred to the sermon as a script.

What I saw in front of me was not robes. What a saw across the stage was not a crucifix.

The all new Precious Heart wore a simple white sheath dress. Her feet were bare. Today, her hair was jet black and held back in a ponytail. She wore no makeup as far as I could tell. Across the stage, Precious had set up a mannequin and a table laid out with cosmetics and jewelry. I had seen the sermon. I knew the topic of discussion, but I wasn't exactly sure how this played in with the props.

I took a deep breath and decided to have

faith. With a smile that I suspected looked more nervous than reassuring, I sent Precious out on stage.

Now, dwarfs are not particularly plenty in the United States Midwest. In fact, there are only like thirty thousand people afflicted with dwarfism in the entire United States. Many in the congregation had probably never seen a woman of Precious Heart's statute anywhere other than on TV or in the movies. The mumbled conversation was audible. Some giggles and out and out laughter spotted the crowd as well.

Precious must have been accustomed to this kind of reception. She stood patiently with her head held high until the people quieted.

"Good morning. My name is Guide Precious Heart."

Her voice held a lyrical quality that I had never heard before. She looked so small up on that stage. So small and innocent and yet oddly she owned the stage as well as if she were not one woman but an entire choir of saintly voices.

"Today, I come to you as the newest member of this congregation. I come to you alone and bare of embellishments, of camouflage, of adornment. You see me as I really am. A lonely soul who seeks a higher power to envelop me in love, beauty and, yes, wealth."

Precious strolled across the stage as she spoke to the audience, her manner as soothing as if she were speaking to one special friend rather than a room of strangers.

"I come to you with the desire to not lead you into greatness, but to walk with you. Together we will walk the sacred path." She reached for the gladiator's sandals beside the mannequin and carried them to the edge of the stage. She sat down with her legs over the edge. She wiggled her bare toes. "We will dip our feet into the eternal river of life and luxuriate as the cool water refreshes us. We will rejuvenate our souls. But when we are done, when we are done, we will put on our shoes..." She slipped on the sandals and buckled them as she spoke. "...because we will need protection along the stony path leading us from poverty to the golden gates of success." She stood and walked from one side of the stage to the other, making sure everyone saw the shoes. "Just like these shoes protect my feet from stones, the

Church of Perpetual Profits will protect you from stumbling, from falling into a life destitute of fellowship and wealth. A life not worth living, if you ask me. *I* will walk beside you and steady you when you falter. All you have to do is ask. All you have to do is reach out and take my hand as a friend.

She returned to the mannequin and removed the brightly gemmed collar from its neck and placed it around her neck. The collar was wide enough to cover her shoulders and hung down over her breasts. "Together, we will adorn ourselves with all the riches this world has to offer, but first we must do the work and learn the discipline necessary to turn coal into diamonds." She slipped rings on her fingers and a gold braided belt around her waist.

"We must build our wealth one item at a time, the way an artist layers paint on a canvas. One layer is simple. The next adds wide strokes of an idea. With each additional layer, the artist defines the wide strokes into a complicated piece of work. It means something different to each person who views it, but everyone agrees it is a masterpiece. In reality, it's the same way we dress ourselves day after day. We put on our clothes one item at a time, then we accentuate our assets with jewels and accessories." She showed the congregation her hands and arms, now heavy with rings and bracelets.

She sat down at the table laden with cosmetics and a tall black woman in a traditional African dashiki padded barefoot onto the stage. She artfully applied the cosmetics to the plain face of Precious Heart, carefully working from one side and then the other without blocking the congregation's view of their new leader.

"And as we prosper, we will show the world what it is to be kings and queens. We will shower or friends and family with love and gifts. We will give back to the Church what it has given to us, and we will pray for the strength to lead the lives of royalty with grace."

Precious was no longer a simple woman on an empty stage. Her eyes were heavily lined with kohl. Her eye shadow mimicked the brilliance of her collar. The African woman placed a blunt cut wig upon her head and topped the wing with a headpiece that was almost as tall as the woman wearing it.

Precious stood. Where once a proud but plain woman stood, meek and unassuming, now a powerful leader of men ruled.

Precious raised her hands slowly, palms up toward the ceiling. "Now rise, my kings and queens, greet the people around you as equals and thank them for helping you along your journey."

I peeked around the curtain and was stunned to see the love in the audience. Men and women were shaking hands. Smiles were eager and many were looking at Precious as if she were a goddess.

Who would have thought the same woman I had conned into dressing like a bird for the *Save a tree, file electronically* campaign could elicit such a reaction from a crowd. She was a many-facetted gem in a small human body.

I looked to see what Janet's reaction was to what we had seen. She was crying. Her head high and her face as at peace as I had seen it in a long time.

When Janet saw me staring, she said, "We will succeed now. This was the missing element."

Francine Zane

Chapter 24: Do You?

I could finally take a breath without worrying about how much it was costing me. Precious Heart followed up her first sermon with six more just as successful. Profits were up two hundred percent, even with the black hole of a gravy kitchen eating into our earnings. The upcharges weren't paying off as well as I'd hoped. Next week, we were adding rum balls to the menu. Rum balls ought to go over well with a demographic made up largely of addicts.

Next week, we were holding our first ever exorcism. Mother Superior Tracillia had agreed we could use her private chapel for the ceremony in exchange for additional funds. Apparently four children weren't enough for the woman. Now she wanted to hire Jake and Maxi, during Maxi's off hours from the Church, of course, to go into the Forbidden Zone and pull out three more children. One of the congregation had approached her about neglected grandchildren, so now we were in the search and rescue business. I was still working on how to make that a profit center. I really needed to get a handle on all these side projects, but it was hard to say no to a woman with a ruler.

When I heard a knock at my office door, I called out, "Come in!"

Buff Bronzebutt did not enter my office. That would have been understating the occasion. No, Buff filled the office as surely as a laughing gas fills the world with happiness. Actually, it was better than that. Think of being alone in a room with Buff Bronzebutt like being trapped in an elevator of laughing gas with a dozen male underwear models, all dressed for their next big shoot. Even better, the elevator jostles you into the arms of the best-looking model, and he holds you while staring deep into your eyes and asking, "Are you alright," and then—

"Are you alright?" Buff asked for what I gathered was at least the second time.

"Yes, sure. What can I do to you...I mean for you...I mean...?" I cleared my dry throat from all those words I was tripping over.

"Are you looking for Janet? I can go get her." I offered as I darted toward the door, careful to leave lots of space between Buff and me lest I fall or something.

He motioned me to relax. "No, I'm here to see you. I was hoping you could give me some advice."

I stopped and made an about face. "Me?" I squeaked.

"Yeah. Can we sit?"

I nodded and led him to the couch and offered him coffee. I'm not sure why. I doubt we had any made. Luckily, he declined.

"You know I love Janet, right?"

I nodded.

"I've been in love with her since forever. I'd like to marry her but she keeps turning me down, you know?"

"Yeah, and I have to say your last proposal was amazing. Far more romantic than many marriages, actually."

"Thanks. That is kind of why I'm here. I've run out of ideas. I've gotten down on one knee. I've proposed with song, in my skivvies, with a skywriter, beneath the ocean, with a ring hidden in a baked potato. I don't recommend that one, by the way. Darn near blistered my fingers pulling that thing out of the potato after she turned me down. I've proposed by mail, email, voicemail. I had a singing Valentine sing my proposal to her over the JumboTron at a baseball game. I hired a mariachi band to accompany me while I proposed here at work.

"I've proposed while flying into a breathtaking sunset, on a vacation to the tropics, during a weekend at a bed and breakfast. I had a flash mob propose for me at the Home Depot, and an Italian opera singer sang my proposal during a matinee movie. I tried to hire Patrick Swayze to reenact the *Ghost* pottery scene with her, but he is kind of, you know, dead.

"Daddy B says I've spent more on trying to get this woman to marry me than some third world countries spend on health care of an entire year. Don't get me wrong. She's worth every penny of it! But, man, a guy can only take so much rejection."

The man looked defeated. His shoulders were slumped. That dynamic smile I had admired so often from afar was missing, and he looked oddly pale under that tropical tan he maintained. I felt for him. I couldn't think of another man who had gone so far out of his way to make a woman love him. But what could I say? *Hey, Buff, your crazy woman won't marry you because your dad has blackmailed her into saying no. Oh, by the way, the dumbass kid that ruined your mother's funeral is your son. Janet got pregnant and gave up the baby without ever telling you. Your dad knows, though.* Yeah, that would go over about as well as my fat ass over a ten-foot fence.

"Have you tried talking to her?" I asked.

"About what?"

Really?

"About why she won't marry you?"

"Oh, that. Yeah, I guess."

Buff looked confused, as if I had asked him how to build a house without walls or a roof. In a way, I had. Building a marriage without the walls of communication doesn't make for a very solid structure. I had to wonder how much Janet and Buff really talked. Sure, he gave her things and did things for her, but how often did he talk to her about what she wanted, what she thought? It wasn't any of my business any more than how to get her to marry him, still everyone wanted a happily ever after, and Janet deserved one.

"How about talking her into marriage therapy?" I asked, reaching for a way to open the lines of communication between them. I knew Janet had secrets to tell him. He likely had secrets as well.

"We're not even married yet! Wouldn't that be putting the cart before the horse?"

"Well, I mean relationship therapy. Something to help you get Janet to open up to you and talk."

"If she really loved me, she would just marry me." The defeated Buff looked a lot less attractive when he pouted.

"She might see it as if you really loved her, being married really wouldn't matter."

We both fell silent for a bit. I could tell Buff was trying to wrap his mind around what I said, but it wasn't coming to him easily. I didn't feel comfortable saying anymore. In fact, I would have loved him to leave. Slowly, so I could watch the show but leave nonetheless.

"I know!" Buff jumped up and rubbed his hands together. "I got it. I'll buy her a Maserati—a red one. She likes red. And I'll slip the ring on the key chain and give it to her for her birthday with a big red—no, too much red—white bow on the car! I'll invite our entire high school graduating class to the party. You can come, too! This will be great!"

Buff took me by both hands and swung me around and then enveloped me in a bear hug tight enough to take my breath away. Yea me! The most physical contact I'd had in months and it was with my partner's boyfriend.

As Buff flew out of my office on winged feet, I considered hightailing it to Janet's office to find out why she had not cleared the air with Buff. None of my business. None of my business. Definitely none of my business.

I continued my mantra of not my business as I strolled across the hall and tapped on Janet's door, then let myself in.

"You haven't talked to him yet, have you?"

"Sure, come on in without waiting for an invite," Janet said. "And hello! What are you talking about?"

She looked over half-lensed reading glasses at me.

"Buff. He was just in my office asking about proposing to you again."

The glasses came off faster than Clark

Kent during his best metamorphoses into Superman. "You told him not to bother, didn't you?"

"Um, no. Why haven't you talked to him?"

"What if I said it just never came up?"

"Janet! This is important stuff here. Are you telling me you couldn't make the subject come up?"

"Well, maybe...okay! You've got me. I'm a coward. A sniveling coward."

"The man plans to buy you a Maserati, for Christ's sake! You've got to tell him."

"Fine. I'll tell him. Tonight, but I'm still not marrying him."

"Can I have the Maserati then?"

"No, you can't have the Maserati."

I snapped my fingers. "Damn."

Chapter 25: Monkey Boy

"Monkey fuzzy butt!" I called out after adding up the same list of numbers for the third time and coming up with a different answer than the last two.

"Excuse me?" said tall, dark and handsome from my doorway.

I jumped up and spilled my coffee. "Shit!" I grabbed a facial tissue from the smartly colored box on my desk and began mopping up the mess. Yeah, saying shit in front of a stranger was way more professional than monkey fuzzy butt.

The stranger disappeared and returned with a handful of paper towels, presumably from the restroom down the hall.

"Here, let me help."

"Thanks," I said.

We worked well together and soon had salvaged most of the papers on my desk. I dropped the last of the wet towels in the trash, then offered my guest an antibacterial hand wipe.

"I'm sorry about that," I apologized while we cleaned our hands. "How can I help you?"

"I was hoping you could help me file some back tax returns," he said with a smile that almost brought me to my knees.

"Well, that isn't really what we do anymore, sort of." How to describe Church of Perpetual Profits to an outsider? I held out a hand. "I'm Lolla Brigida, by the way. And you are?"

He shook my hand. "My name is Monk Boyd."

His hand was warm and strong. I know I held on longer than I should, but after the Buff incident, I was hyperaware of just how little physical contact I allowed in my life. Eventually, though, I had to let go or pay rent on the palm space.

"So how can I help you, Mr. Boyd?" I repeated without thinking about it as I offered him a seat in the visitor's chair. What can I say? My mind was on his brown eyes and messily sexy hairdo. I was so proud of myself for not having my mind on other parts of him until I realized I was repeating myself.

I sat down in my desk chair and jumped back up again, then dropped back down. The coffee had dripped in my seat, and I hadn't realized it until I sat in it. Now to stand up would mean proving to Monk Boyd that not only was I clumsy, but I also wet my pants on occasion. Joy. I made a mental note to buy a new chair with a super absorbent seat, just in case.

"You okay? You look a little...um...uncomfortable," Monk said.

"Yes, sure. Just...an old hip injury flaring up. I played...ah...tetherball as a kid and took a bad spill one day. Haven't been the same since." Tetherball? Really? Well, it was the closest thing to a sport that I ever played. I was more of a math club kind of girl.

Monk nodded. "Yeah, I have an old knee injury from college that I have to work around."

"Football?" I asked.

"No. I tripped falling down from the second-floor window of our frat house into a Jell-O pit."

"Wow, sounds painful," I said.

"Not until the alcohol wore off." Monk smiled, and I heard Marvin Gaye serenading me about the healing benefits of sex.

"Ah, I guess we all did foolish things in college. Good thing we outgrow them as we get older."

"Yeah, I guess so."

I worked hard at not asking how I can help him again. "So, Mr. Boyd, you are looking for a tax preparer?"

"Yeah, I kind of got behind on my taxes, and now my girlfriend wants us to buy a house together. The bank won't give us a loan until I file all my past tax returns."

Boo! I felt the air go out of my boobs, and my wet seat just didn't matter anymore.

"How did you get behind?" I asked. I'm not sure why. I wasn't in the tax preparation business anymore. I was in the religion business.

"Well, it started about six years ago, I guess. I was boogie boarding my way across the Pacific to China. I ran out of steam about halfway there, and I had to stop on Maui for a few years. Have you ever been to Maui?"

I shook my head no. "Always meant to go but never found the time."

"Well, it is totally awesome. They have these like Hawaiian babes there who do nothing but bring you these fruity drinks. I don't think I sobered up for at least six months. By the time I did, I couldn't remember where I was headed, so I just stayed another year and worked in the pineapple fields, slept on the beach, surfed and pumped weight. That's how I got this."

He pulled the skin tight t-shirt over his head. I had a front row seat to the unveiling of a beautifully sculpted six pack. Then he turned around and pointed to a large ugly scar running from his left shoulder blade down to his right hip.

"Oh my, that looks awful. What happened?" Such a sad flaw on such a lovely canvas. I felt steam building up from my wet seat and felt the need to fan myself but refrained.

Monk continued. "I was spotting for a wahine while she was doing a bench press set, only I didn't know she belonged to some mammoth who doesn't like to share. Anyway, he thought I was infringing on his territory and beat me black and blue with a sweat-soaked towel. That scar is what is left of a six-week hospital stay and months of physical therapy. The hospital staff said it was the first major towel snapping injury they had ever seen. Go figure.

"So after that, I made my way back to the mainland and opened a party shop with a buddy, and that was great for a while. We would basically go into anywhere at any time and turn blah into an instant party with booze, broads—excuse me—women, music, decorations, food, party favors of sorts, whatever the customer wanted."

"And still no tax returns?" I asked.

Monk nodded. "I'm getting to that. So, at the end of the first year, I'd taken my information into the Shameless Rat Bastards office, then I headed out to do a job. This job was for a bunch of tweens. The parents hired us to set up a party that was a cross between *Hunger Games* and a typical paintball party. My part in the party was to drop the beehive at midnight. Of course, the bees were the stingerless kind, or so I was told when I rented them.

"As you may have figured out by now, I'm not the luckiest man. I was nearing the top of the tree with the beehive tucked into a sling on my back. I went to climb out on the tree limb where I'd planned to make my drop when a group of six or so tween girls thought it would be fun to shoot their paint guns at me. A magenta-filled ball slapped me between the eyes blinding me and throwing me off balance.

"Down I fell, beehive and all. That is when I found out stingless bees don't really exist. Go figure, huh?" Monk leaned forward with his elbows on his knees, his forgotten t-shirt a wad of red cloth in his hands.

"I had no idea."

I was beginning to wonder if I was on Candid Camera, and the world was waiting to find out how big a tale Monk could sell me before I called bullshit.

"How bad were you hurt?" I asked.

"Well, the fall broke both of my legs, but that was nothing compared to what those girls did to me." He leaned back again and stretched those long legs out before him, drawing my attention to the neon yellow running shoes that he wore with no socks. "After the bees cleared the area, the girls decided to use eyebrow tweezers and cuticle scissors to remove the hundreds of stingers from my face and body before slathering me with mud. Later, my sister found a picture they had posted on Facebook of me covered with flowers as the girls circled me dancing a happy dance. Do you want to see?"

He pulled out his android phone and pulled up the picture before handing it to me. I couldn't really make out who was covered in mud and white daisies, but it did sort of resemble a human.

"Wow, tween girls did that to you?" I asked.

"Yeah. I lay there for like three hours before my partner found me and called an ambulance. The parents, my clients, wouldn't let the EMTs in until the party ended the next morning, though. On the upside, they did slip me a morphine cocktail, so I slept through the pajama party, bonfire and eventual beheading of my partner.

"I swear *Hunger Games* is a tween handbook to murder and mayhem. I can't believe parents let kids read that stuff. Anyway, I was in the hospital for a long time, and when I got out SRB had closed up shop. I couldn't even get my docs back."

It was getting dark outside, so I decided I had better curtail more of his year-by-year account, but I had to admit, this guy was making falling on a penis look good in so many ways.

"So what about this year. Why didn't you

file this year?" I asked.

"Ah well, I got together with some of my old college buddies. We were having some brews and reliving old times. The next thing I knew, I'd take Kyle and Dipper up on a dare. They'd found a nest of poisonous spiders and dared me to wade through them barefoot." He shook his head. "I never could turn down a good dare, so I had a few more beers, took off my shoes and socks and rolled up my pants legs because I had no desire to have a poisonous spider climb up my pants leg and bite me on my gonads or something. I did pretty good, too, until a particularly large spider bit me on my big toe, then I flinched and about two dozen other spiders decided to join in the human flesh feast. Man, I gotta tell you. Poisonous spider bites sting but not as bad as the infection that I got later. The infection made me so sick that I had to go to the emergency room, again.

"By now, all the hospital staff knew me, and I had a permanent reservation on a nice little corner gurney. After a couple of weeks as an inpatient and two near death experiences—I can tell you about those another time if you want—they sent me home with a topical salve I was supposed to doctor my bites with. I guess they didn't get all the poison and infection out of my toes because one day I was doctoring my feet when I had an intolerable itch in my left ear. I scratched my ear, and the next morning, my ear was swollen shut and full of pus."

"You did what?" I asked as I squirmed against the wet leather desk chair. This story was beyond belief, and I had the overwhelming desire to change my clothes before I developed adult diaper rash.

"I'd transferred the poison from my foot to my ear. For the next few days, I ran a fever like crazy, was delusional and in so much pain that I wished for the good old days when all I had to worry about was beestings and two broken legs. By the time I recovered, April 15 had passed, and I was worried about more immediate things like getting back to work so I could pay my rent and car payment."

"Is this a joke?" I asked. No one could have that kind of bad luck.

"Cross my heart, ma'am, I'm telling the truth. Now all I need is a little help to get in good with the IRS, and maybe I can rebuild my life."

I looked at him for a long time, trying my best to keep my eyes on his face, but his shirt was still off, and that made it hard. Buff Bronzebutt looked good, but this guy, well there was something about him that made it hard not to just eat him up. Maybe it was because he was clumsier than I was. Of course, the six pack abs didn't hurt...or the long legs...well that cutie-pie smile was awfully nice too...

"So do you think you can help me?"

I couldn't believe I was going to say this, but here it went, "Well, Shyster and Shyster is no longer in business, but my partner and I do some charity work at the Church of Perpetual Profits. We can fit you in for an initial consultation on Thursday—at no charge, of course."

I smiled as I chanted in my head, *I hate myself. I hate myself. I hate myself.*

Francine Zane

Chapter 26: Drunk Baby

"You did what?" Janet asked.

"I took on a client as part of our free tax services. I figured if everyone else was giving away our money, I might as well get in on the action. We can set aside so many hours of free services a month as part of our cover as a non-profit," I reasoned, hoping she would buy the ancillary reason for my actions.

"Sure, that's the reason. What is his name?"

I looked at the preliminary information sheet I had Monk fill out before he left. "Monk E. Boyd."

Janet laughed. "Our new client is Monkey Boy."

"No, that's not what I said." I grin played at my lips, though, as I imagined him climbing the tree hand over hand as his tight little butt...what a nice little butt so taut in those faded jeans..."

"Lolla!" Janet's grin got bigger. "You like this guy don't you? I can tell by that flush in your cheeks."

"No! I can't. He has a girlfriend. They are getting married soon! He told me."

Aw, honey." Janet patted me on the back. "What dumb luck. The first guy you've shown any interest in since I've known you, and he is practically married."

I stared at my toes as if I was trying to see spider poison beneath the luscious raspberry nail polish. I might as well be staring at the wall to find out what time it is from the clock in the next room. When I looked up again, Janet was gone, and I was left alone pouting over a stranger's good luck. Monkey Boy—see now Janet's got me calling him that—might as will be some movie star on the big screen. Both were unapproachable. Miles, security guards, lifestyles and that little thing called reality stood between the movie star and me. And the fiancée stood between me and Monkey Boy. Well, that and with his luck combined with mine, the very real possibility we would kill each other purely by accident.

As if my attitude didn't suck bad enough, I had the pleasure of meeting the girlfriend at any time now. I really didn't want to meet her, to have her happiness rubbed into my face, and if she turned out to be a blonde bimbette with perfect hair and perfect teeth who wore a size negative two, I would likely scream or kill her outright.

I didn't have time to decide on a course of action before Janet showed up with the woman in question. Standing about my height, the brunette looked like she was about twelve months pregnant with twins. I had a hard time not thinking of the twins as already half grown with full sets of teeth and angry dispositions, kind of like their mom. Was it that wrong of me to hope the delivery would be really, really painful?

"I'm Sar Rah. Monk asked me to bring these to you." She thrust a fistful of papers to me. "He said you were helping him get is life in order or something."

"Thanks." I took the papers, which consisted of a few cash register receipts, a single rumpled sheet from a legal pad and a couple of W-2s that resembled used tissue more than tax documents. Not much to show for six years of a man's life. "And congratulations on the new house."

"What house?"

"Monkey—I mean Monk—" I had to watch that. "Monk said you were buying a house together."

"He said what? You've got to be kidding. Any man who thinks that just because he knocked me up with a drunk baby means we are a couple has got to be crazy."

I had only thought she looked angry before. That must have been her happy face.

"Oh, I'm sorry. I hope the baby will be okay."

"Why wouldn't he? I'm a good mother. I don't need no man to raise a baby."

"Well, you said drunk baby. I assumed you meant your baby has fetal alcohol syndrome..."

"Do I look like an idiot to you?"

Sar Rah was in my face now. I could smell the pickles on her breath.

"But you said..."

"What I said was I am having a drunk baby. You know, a baby that was conceived when I had too many beers and fell onto the first available penis I found. I stopped drinking as soon as I realized I was pregnant. Sheesh. You must be as dumb as Monk if you think I'd ever hurt my baby."

Sar Rah ran a comforting hand over her filled-to-bursting form.

Actually, I did feel like I'd lost a few IQ points since Sar Rah had entered the room, but I was willing to give up IQ points if what she was saying was true. If Monkey Boy was actually available, I had a chance for a personal life. It had been so long since I'd had a personal life, not a real one.

I wet my lips and asked the question that was hanging out there. "So, you and Monk aren't a couple?"

"For Christ's sake no! Monk is bad mojo. Anyone who hooks up with him is in a world of hurt for the rest of her life, I can tell you that for sure! He dated my roommate in college, and the next thing I knew, she was convicted of peddling drugs, and they weren't even her drugs. They were mine! A year later, a girl I worked with went out for coffee with him and lost her virginity with the Starbucks' barista. Can you imagine? That's like losing your virginity to a freaking janitor. No one wants it to go that way.

"All I did was sleep with him. I imagine I'll get off easy and die during childbirth or something."

"Oh, I'm sure he's not that bad."

Sar Rah looked at me a long moment. "You got the hots for him, don't you? You've let that kick ass body talk to you. Geez, I thought you accounting types had more sense than that."

I blinked back whatever might have been showing on my face. "It's not like that. He's just led such an exciting life that I'm interested in his story."

"My advice for you, sister, is to run far and run fast, as fast as you can and as far as you can. Just like I am as soon as I have this baby. That man is toxic." She shrugged. "But it's your life. Do what you want.

"Hey, I've got to go. I'm the designated driver tonight. It takes a lot of time to make this..." She ran a hand from her face down toward her feet. "...party ready."

She waddled out the door and was gone just like that and, along with her, so was my depression. Which left room for the whopper guilt that strolled right in and made itself at home in my psyche. What was I thinking! You don't get involved with clients, even free clients. It was a cardinal rule. The ethical issues were insurmountable. Besides, Monkey Boy was younger than I and obviously fell more than I did. How could we hold each other up like couples were supposed to do if we were both flying in the wind?

I decided to take a walk around the Church property and clear my head only my feet kept taking me back to Mother Superior Tracillia's private chapel. I finally gave in and peeked inside. There she was with her head bent over hands cupped in prayer. I briefly wondered if she had thought about the fact that the red soles of her Louboutin's belied her self-imposed vow of poverty. On the upside, if the IRS took everything we owned, she could just sell some shoes to support the orphanage.

Man, I had to stop thinking this way. Success bred success. Skepticism bred ingrown toenails and failure. Besides, if I were to believe my clients, the IRS had ways of knowing. They could get into people's brains and search out every last tax infraction even thought of in the last twenty years. I had to think positive thoughts like we are perfectly legitimate or we were doomed.

"Come in, my daughter," Tracillia said without looking up. "I'm almost done here."

I took a seat on one of the hard benches

and waited, my hands clasped in my lap. Here I was half owner of a church, and this was the first time I had actually sat on one of the benches. I was always so busy helping orchestrate the show that I never took the time to enjoy it, and yet I sometimes wondered if this place was changing me more than I had changed it.

The Mother finished her prayers and joined me. We sat in silence for a while before she said, "You are troubled, my child. How can I help you?"

"I'm not...okay yes, I guess I am troubled...sort of...maybe or maybe I'm just having a bad day." A tear slipped down my cheek.

She took my hands in hers. "Is this about the Church? Or the bible? I am almost done with the rough draft, I think. Janet convinced me the copyright is expired on the King James version of the Holy Bible, so we are keeping much of the original wording, especially from the old testament..."

"No, no. It's nothing like that. I'm just having an issue with a client."

"Tell me about it."

I told her about Monk Boyd and a bit

more about myself than I was really comfortable sharing. It's not easy confessing to a nun that you are the bastard child of a bastard child, and you had the hots for a guy who was leaving another woman with a bastard child. That is not the way the world is supposed to go. Somewhere down the line, every family should be able to pinpoint a stabilizing force. Just one person or one couple who had it together long enough to instill a moral compass in the rest of the line. I never felt like I had that. I felt all I had was crazy. Crazy and accident prone did not make for good stability.

"Have you ever considered that perhaps Mr. Boyd is possessed by a demon such as a puck, poltergeist or imp? In fact, from what you have told me, it is just as likely you are possessed as well. I'd guess a poltergeist of some sort that has been passed on from parent to child for generations."

"I'm not so sure I believe in demons." I took back my hand as I slid across the bench away from her a bit. To say I was a bit disconcerted to have left children with this woman was an understatement.

"My dear, how can you believe in the angels of heaven if you do not believe in the demons of hell? The world is full of good and evil. Some are more accepted as normal than others, but both are still very real in this world and in the next."

"Sometimes things just happen. Kind of like winning the lottery or getting run over by a car," I said.

"Not usually. Sometimes things happen because they are God's will, but often the bad things we see in this world are the fault of earthbound demons. I tell you what, let me tell you a story about a girl named Traci." Tricillia smiled, her eyes twinkled enough for me know the Traci in the story was her.

"When I was a girl, I had horrible nightmares. I would wake up screaming, and my pillow would be soaked with my tears. Eventually, my dreams became walking nightmares. I would literally leave my bed and follow the apparitions out of the room and sometimes out the house. Twice, my mother found me in the middle of the street sleeping, and we lived on a busy street. Eventually, my parents were forced to lock me in my room at night. It was the only way to keep me safe, but that was a short-term solution. I began having daydreams at school that were just as horrifying as my night dreams. I would see dead people roaming the halls and weirdly misshapen demons followed around certain people.

"You would be amazed who rated a demon and who didn't. Some of the quietest, kindest people I knew had demons tripping them, leading them the wrong way down a one-way street, spiking their milk with sleeping powder. So much was always happening that only I could see. Me! Some little nobody who could no longer sleep.

"My parents took me to doctors, psychologists, psychiatrists, herbal remedy specialists—just about anybody they could think of who might make me normal. Nothing helped. Well, that isn't true. I finally stopped telling them what I saw. That helped them a little, but they could still tell that I wasn't well.

"Finally, my church minister suggested a pray in. Do you know what a pray in is?"

I shook my head no.

"Well, it is kind of like a Catholic exorcism, but instead of a priest and perhaps one or two other people trying to drive a demon out of a possessed person, the whole congregation comes together. For three nights and two days, they prayed over me, held me, made me pray. And then it happened. It's hard to explain, but it felt like a pop, as if I was encased in a balloon that I had to struggle to breathe through had broken, and I was free. I saw nothing but what everyone else saw, and I could sleep! For the first time in my life, I could sleep without waking up in fear."

"That isn't anything like what I feel, or Monk, if I had to guess. He didn't look as if much scared him really."

"I understand that. My demon was likely a nightmare. That is a demon that comes to you in the night and uses fear to terrorize its victims. Your demons would rather use pain and humiliation to torture you."

I'd spent an entire lifetime trying to outrun clumsy. Gymnastics classes as a child hadn't helped. Neither had dance lessons as a teenager. Age certainly hadn't helped matters. I was three gray hairs and a sagging bottom away from senior citizenship and a broken hip. I could go ahead and buy the walker or try something new to break my hex, and if it worked for me, I might be able to talk Monk into my new cure. In the meantime, I could see his tax returns taking an long time to prepare and requiring a lot of one-on-one meetings. Yeah, I might be attracted to Monkey Boy, but I wasn't crazy. I want to know a man before I put my hooks into him.

Francine Zane

Chapter 27: Exorcize This

How do you dress for an exorcism especially if you are the demon-inflicted victim? Does one dress for comfort or class? Should the clothes be ectoplasm friendly, or should I wear the traditional white nightgown? I flipped through my wardrobe and passed on suits and skirts. I dismissed the binding jeans and briefly considered my fat jeans. I settled on some worn-soft capris, a form-fitting t-shirt and these cute sandals I picked up on sale and never worn before. I figured if I destroyed my clothes, the t-shirt would be tough to tear. I'd already gotten a lot of use out of the capris, and I wouldn't miss shoes that I had so far never found a reason to wear.

We decided to hold the exorcism in Mother Superior's personal chapel. I think she was kind of hoping we would destroy it and give her an excuse to redecorate. She had told me once that she never got the

Black Sabbath vibes out of the place.

Janet picked me up at my place, and we drove to the church in silence. Guide Precious Heart, Mother Tracillia, Jake and—surprise, surprise—Andrew Ren!

"Andrew? What are you doing here?" I asked.

"Didn't I tell you? I changed majors, again. This time, I'm going for a philosophy and religious studies major." He nodded his head toward Precious. "She hired me as an intern!"

The perpetual student has struck again!

"Welcome back into the fold, Andrew." I looked at Tracillia and Precious, anxious to get started. "So, how does this go?"

The women looked at one another and then back at me. Precious spoke up, "Well, we will play it by ear. This is a new religion here, and as you know, Traci is still writing the manual." She nodded toward Jake the Snake and then Andrew Ren. "I invited Jake and Andrew as a precautionary measure. We don't want you to hurt yourself in the process. Is that okay?"

I couldn't see how Andrew would help much. Even now, his attention had drifted off to texting on his android phone, but Jake was a comfort. Jake would protect me, even from myself.

"Sure, sure. What do I do?"

Precious led me to a table set up with six glasses and several bottles of sacramental wine. Beside the wine were two more bottles of rum and a bottle of vodka. She pulled out a chair and beckoned me to sit. For safety, Jake strapped me in with bungee cords around me waist and below my breasts. I tried to tilt the chair to see how stable it was, and it hardly budged.

Precious inspected my bonds and nodded in satisfaction. "Now we drink."

For two and half hours, we sat around the table and drank, then Precious broke out in song while Andrew spit a downbeat. I couldn't join in much, of course. Every time I tried, someone urged me to take another drink. After about the fifth time of undoing my bungee cords so I could drain the—what is the opposite of a snake?—Precious decided we should move the party to the floor. Can't fall on the floor, right?

And then the fun began. The world was moving at a different speed than I was. I was forever jerking myself up from a tilt, and I could no longer find my mouth with the cup.

Precious handed me a sippy cup with an extra-long straw and I continued, wondering when the exorcism would begin because there were way too many people in the room now. There was Janet, sitting in the corner. She looked like she needed another drinky-poo. And little Precious and big Jake and Jake's little friend. If I squinted my face up into a prune, I could just make out the fella's beady little eyes and crooked nose. He smelled, too. Like purple. He waved at me. I tried to wave back, but my hand was busy holding my butt.

Mother Tracillia looked on disapprovingly. Silly me for thinking she carried a ruler. That was no ruler. That was Gertrude, the sneaky little squiggly thing. I used to know her species but I forgot.

"Oh, Gertie," I sang. "You live with a nun."

"What's she talking about?" Andrew asked as he tried to stare a line between me and whatever I was looking at that he couldn't see.

I giggled and lay down. Wow! I could feel the world turning on its axis. I'd better hold on or I'd fall off. I rolled over and pressed myself to the floor, running my hands back and forth, looking for a handhold. If I fell off the world, I'd never get lucky with Monkey Boy. What was the point of going through this if I would still be alone when it was all said and done? I was tired of alone. I wanted to come home to someone who asked about my day and who would keep my feet warm at night.

Beside me, a tribble sidestepped beside me, then it shivered and where there was one tribble, now there were two. Their bodies shook as if they were laughing at me, and I giggled. Better that they laugh with me instead of at me.

Tribbles are a *Star Trek* creation that appeared to be cute balls of fur and made people happy until they didn't. The tribbles reproduced like bunny rabbits on fast forward. Now, that might not sound so bad unless you are on a spaceship with limited storage space. When the storage space runs out, then the tribbles make new dwellings in places like vents, airshafts and electrical equipment. Eventually, those soft, cuddly creatures take over the entire spaceship leaving absolutely no room for anything else like walking and breathing.

I made a mental note to pay the light bill

because it was growing dim in here, and the sound was way too low.

From the distance, the last thing I heard was the distorted words that sounded like, "Shore reading."

Sounded like a plan to me.

Chapter 28: Monkey Love Rescue

I woke up in the daylight in my bed. The sheets were smooth and smelled of lavender. My body ached, but the air felt different as if someone had it professionally cleaned and piped back into my lungs. I was more relaxed than I had ever been in my entire life.

"You're awake," Janet said from somewhere to my left.

I turned my head. "What happened?"

Janet looked everywhere but at my eyes. "I don't want to talk about it. Ever."

"Was it that bad?"

"It was...bizarre...that's all I'll say on the subject. That was my first and last exorcism."

I felt guilty. I didn't know what had happened, but if it made her this uncomfortable, well Janet just didn't deserve this.

I forced my head to nod. "Did it work?"

"I don't know," Janet took a deep breath and let it out, "but we put everything we had into it. Now you are supposed to just rest for a day or two. I've got to go into work for a while, but Precious should be here in a bit to check on you. She said if you didn't wake up by the time she arrived, she would call a doctor."

"Glad it didn't come to that."

"Yeah, me too."

Janet left me alone to rest, but I really didn't feel like resting. I felt like taking a jog, in the rain, with my eyes closed, preferably in traffic. If I could manage to do that and not slip and fall, break an ankle, stumble off the side of the road or get run over, I'd be satisfied that my clumsy streak was over, and I would consider myself truly blessed. Thinking back on the exorcism and the shaken Janet at my bedside, I knew I was blessed if I could even get out of bed without falling. Not many people would go through so much for a friend. Honestly, I didn't even think of them as friends until now. Maybe because I had collected so many acquaintances during my life and so few friends.

I couldn't lay there anymore. I had to get

up. To see what damage was done to my body. I slowly sat up and put one leg over the side of the bed, then the other. Supporting my weight with my hands, I stepped down and felt...nothing. Well, nothing more than I was supposed to. I walked into the bathroom and took a look over and under my clothes. No unusual bruises that weren't there before. No scars. No tattoos. No abnormal growths. My boobs were still hanging low, and my nose was still too pointy.

I was picking at a blackhead behind one knee when I heard someone clear her throat from the open bathroom door. I twisted around from where I had one leg propped up on the edge of the bathtub to see Precious leaning against the doorframe with a quirky grin on her face. That I didn't fall on my face was almost as a big a miracle as the fact I hadn't died of embarrassment. I made a dash for my robe as Precious backed out of the room.

Now covered to my chin in terrycloth, I took a deep breath and went out to the living room where Precious had made herself at home on my couch.

"How are you feeling?" Precious asked.

"Embarrassed."

Precious smiled. "That will pass. So, how are you feeling physically?" She asked as she folded her hands in prim and proper style on her lap, which did nothing to downplay her hot pink hair and the fishnet stockings that she wore with a neon blue skater skirt and halter top. The black biker jacket was the only thing remotely conservative about the Church of Perpetual Profit's Guide.

"Pretty good, actually."

"No hangover? No injuries?"

"No and no. How long was I out? Do I want to know what happened?"

"Janet didn't tell you?"

I shook my head. "She seemed kind of shook up."

"Yeah, probably not her cup of tea, but everyone did a great job!"

I hesitated. I wanted to know, sure. But did I really want to know if everyone was so unwilling to talk about it? I opted to ask her if she wanted coffee instead.

"Oh, no. I had my fill hours ago. It's almost six in the evening now."

"I slept all day?"

"Well, more like you passed out the day

before yesterday." Precious shifted in her seat as if she had somewhere else to be.

"Wow! I've never drunk that much before. In fact, I've never drunk enough to pass out. I do know I was seeing some unusual things before I passed out, though."

We discussed the tribbles, Gertrude and Jake's little friend, then Precious decided to fill me in on what I missed.

"Once you passed out, we created a safety circle around you. Mother Traci led us in prayer for a while, but that got boring, so Jake suggested we should take a breather and come back refreshed. The only problem was when we came back, you had locked the door and wouldn't let us in. You kept singing something about troubling tribbles, which makes a lot more sense now. Eventually you got quiet again, and we were concerned you might have knocked yourself out or something, so Jake pulled out his revolver and blew the lock off the door. Afterward, Traci smacked him with the ruler and threatened to tell his mother, then made Janet promise to replace the door with some antique model she found on eBay.

"We found you inside curled up in a fetal

position hugging your shoes. You said the tribbles were out getting a six-pack of oysters and some scrambled ostrich eggs. Then you started crying because you didn't see how they could possibly bring any back for you since they didn't have arms. I have to tell you, Lolla, none of us had any idea what a tribble was. Andrew finally looked it up on his phone, so we at least knew we were looking for alien furballs, but by then, you'd given up crying in Janet's arms and wanted to call Monkey Boy for a sleepover.

"When we tried to talk you out of a midnight hook up with a client, you reverted back to your toddler self and threw a hissy fit."

I vaguely recalled this part. Flashes of me sitting on the floor kicking my feet and pounding my fists into the ground, but mostly the recollection gave me a headache.

"Jake tried to keep you from hurting yourself, but he was already injured from Mother Traci's ruler whack, plus you had a lot of anger built up inside of you. You eventually freed an arm and threw an elbow into his nose. I just got back from visiting him in the hospital."

"Oh no! Is he okay?"

"Well he was an ugly old coot to begin with, and it wasn't his first broken nose, so he doesn't look any worse for wear, other than the nose brace and two black eyes. But he'll need at least two surgeries to remove all the loose cartilage before it travels to his brain and causes brain damage."

"I am so sorry! I would have never hurt Jake." I was ready to die. It was one thing to hurt myself, but I had never in my life hurt another person. I pulled my legs up beneath me and hugged my arms to my body, readying myself for whatever came next.

"Jake knows that. We all do. Anyway, the only way we could calm you down short of a sleep hold, which Traci and Janet both refused to let me put on you, was to call Monkey Boy and invite him to come on down. I've got to hand it to you, he is one fine looking man, and he must think a lot of you. It was about three in the morning by then, and he was there in less than a half hour."

I hid my face in my hands and wished it all away.

Precious continued, "That is when things really got interesting. As soon as you saw Monkey Boy, you burst into tears because you said the tribbles were suffocating him, and they planned to eat his face off. Then you threw yourself at him and started tearing his clothes off. The poor man was naked before we could drag you off him.

"I should thank you for that. He is one of the few men I've ever seen who actually looked better without clothes. Only once you were satisfied that the tribbles weren't eating him, you felt bad that he had nothing to wear and we did.

Precious got to her feet and looked around. "Lolla, you might want a drink for the next part. I know I do. Where do you keep your liquor?"

I pointed her to the kitchen and the liquor supply on the top shelf over the sink. She came back carrying two thirty-two ounce super cups filled with ice and something dark.

She handed me a cup and urged me to drink. One sip and I identified the contents. It was everything on my liquor shelf. I tasted rum, vodka, wine, possibly some peach schnapps and just a very light dash of cola.

"Gag, Precious, what are you trying to do to me?"

"Numb the pain, baby, numb the pain."

She took a huge swig followed by large gulp and let out a big burp. "Sorry about that. Actually, I'm not sure why I'm worried about you. You can't remember any of this. I'm the one who can visualize every last detail of it."

Precious returned to her seat on the sofa and held onto her drink as if it was her lifeline to sanity. "So you were so upset about Monk's naked state..."

"You said that," I said as I guarded myself against what could possibly be worse than what I'd already heard.

Precious continued with her gaze on her drink, "You were so upset that you insisted we all get naked so Monkey Boy wouldn't be embarrassed. The man swore he wasn't embarrassed, but you weren't happy until we were all standing around in our birthday suits. Then you decided the clothes were covered with tribbles and insisted we burn them, even Mother Traci's red soled Louboutin's. The woman cried."

She took another drink while I debated how I could possibly make this up to them. I had a feeling note cards and nice gift baskets wouldn't do the trick.

Precious continued, "Well, apparently the burning of the clothes completed the exorcism. You said all the tribbles were gone, and we were safe to take a nap, then you fell back to sleep."

"Precious, I am so sorry. If there is anything, anything at all I can do to make this up to you..." I was on my feet and pacing a path between my seating area and the front door. I considered just moving to another country and never seeing any of these people again, but I kind of liked this country, besides my lease wasn't up on this place.

Precious waved me off. "Aw, don't worry about it. I've decided to think of it as one of those corporate retreats activities where people go to learn to open up to one another and work better as a team. It's not the first time I've been naked in a room of people, and it likely won't be the last, especially if we offer exorcisms as part of our normal church services." She took another swig of her drink, her words beginning to slur. "What really bothered me was Andrew. That boy looks like an anorexic squirrel naked. And did you know he has a scar right over his tailbone that resembles a tail removal?"

I shuddered at the image.

I thought of another question. "So how

did you get home without any clothes?"

Precious said, "Well Mother Tracillia streaked across the hall and put on some of her own clothes. She brought back some for the rest of us, but she is such a petite little thing. Nothing fit. She ended up bringing us some of the choir robes."

"I hope you cleaned them before returning them to the choir room," I said.

"Lolla, my girl, we burned them. Besides, I was planning to replace the robes with something a bit jazzier. You know, like maybe something Elvis would have worn in Vegas. It's all in the show, you know. I could go on stage and say absolutely nothing for an hour, but as long as I put on a show, they'd keep coming back."

"Whatever works, Precious. Whatever works."

I made a mental note to check into televising her sermons next year. With all the costume changes, Precious was by far the most visually stimulating holy leader I'd ever seen. And who could say no to Elvis costumes, especially after all she had done for me.

Francine Zane

Chapter 29: Taxed to Death

Uh oh. It's not a good sign when Janet is already wearing her serious face before I get through the door good.

"What's up?" I might as well face the music head on.

"I've heard everything now," Janet said.

"What do you mean?"

"Well, Precious had a meeting with one of the congregation this morning. Precious wasn't sure how to deal with the situation the woman was in, so she called me." Janet said.

"Money issues?"

"Well, sort of."

This story was going to take a long time at this rate and my Starbucks non-fat, no foam, decaffeinated, sugar-free excuse for a wake me up was getting cold. "Let me put down my stuff, and you can tell me."

I dropped my stuff off in my office, took a long, careful sip of the coffee and joined

Janet in her office. Her desk was piled monitor high with papers, as usual. The rest of her office was picture perfect, but that desk was a danger zone.

I made myself comfortable in one of her guest chairs and held the coffee between both hands, letting the heat wake me up. "Okay, I'm ready. Give it up."

Janet nodded and clasped her hands together on her desk. "So, this new church member—Della, I think her names is—asked for some spiritual guidance regarding her deceased mother. I guess her mother's body is currently at the Into the Clouds Funeral Home, and Della can't get her buried."

"Ah, so she needs help paying for the funeral?" I deduced.

"No! That was what I thought, too, in the beginning, but strangely that isn't it." Janet said. "Della was upset because the funeral director said he couldn't prepare the body for burial because he had received a hold order from the IRS."

I shook my head and squeezed my eyes shut for a second. "What? The IRS doesn't hold bodies. That is one of the best things about it! You die. You are done. Your estate may have to deal with any outstanding debts, but you're out of the taxability game."

Janet nodded. "That is what I thought, too. As a courtesy, I agreed to speak with the funeral director, and sure enough, he has a warrant to hold the body until the IRS can take a look."

"Does Della have any idea why the IRS is holding the body?"

"Yeah, actually she does. Apparently mom has made a lucrative living over the course of the last thirty years or so by being more than one person. She files a tax return as herself with her Social Security and pension income. She also files a second return as her twin sister who died as an infant. She set up a shield company and issued tax documents in the sister's name, then she takes the tax documents to SRB— thank God it wasn't us—and files for a refund. She also files a return in the name of her son who has been a prisoner of war for the last ten years. Somehow she is drawing disability benefits under his name as well.

"Last month, the IRS caught up with her and was doing a thorough exam of her activities for the last five years. Della thinks that is why her mother died. That her mother overdosed on her medications intentionally. Death seemed preferable to prison, I guess."

"Wow! That's a lot to take in. What does the daughter think we can do for her?" I asked.

Janet took a deep breath and let it out. "Well, she thinks there is a magic form that we can fill out to have her mother's body released. She said she's spent hours out at IRS.gov looking for the form but can't find it. As tax professionals, she thinks we have an in on the body releasing forms."

"And you told her what?"

"I told her I would look into it, and I did," Janet said. "Lolla, I called the IRS and was told that the body would remain on hold until the examination was finished. Poor Della can't bury her mother for what may be months, even if she does cooperate and gives the IRS full access to all of her mother's records.

"In effect, unbeknownst to anyone I know, apparently the IRS can actually follow you into the afterlife and ensure you will not rest in peace until your tax obligations are resolved."

"You know, Janet, this might be a great

opportunity for us," I said as my brain stretched around the new information.

"How so?"

"Well, what if we offered afterlife tax coverage to our church members. You know, a form of insurance to protect them from having their bodies and souls repossessed by the IRS."

"Lolla! You are crazy. We can't guarantee that!"

"No, now wait a second, Janet. Think about it. Between the two of us, we have how many decades of experience dealing with the IRS? Thirty or forty years' worth? How many times have you even heard of the IRS repossessing a body, not to mention how would you prove the IRS repossessed your soul after death?"

"This was a new one for me."

"Exactly. We set a limit on the maximum payout, and we will likely clean up on premiums for years before ever see a claim." I really liked this idea so much better than gravy kitchens and orphans. We could actually make money at this. And I couldn't think of one legal reason we couldn't create this new type of insurance, provided we found an actuary to confirm my suspicions that we would likely never have to pay out, and we complied with the insurance commission's regulations.

"Okay," I said. "You deal with the grieving daughter. I'll come up with a business plan for...what should we call this?"

"Let's keep it simple. We'll call it Afterlife Tax Coverage. Leave it to Precious to find a way to sell it to the congregation. I swear that woman could sell used tampons to menopausal women as a cure for aging."

My eyes lit up as I thought about the possibilities of that suggestion before Janet shot me down with the cold look of a woman who absolutely knew when no was her final answer. I sighed and headed back to my office. I'd fight that battle another day.

Chapter 30: One Million Dollars!

"Lolla!"

"Janet!" I mimicked her startled expression as I jumped up from my seat at my desk.

"We did it!"

"Did what?" I closed my eyes and prayed it wasn't going to cost us more money. I was still cringing at how much the Louboutin's had eaten into my Me account. That poor account was never going to grow big enough to—

"We just crossed the million-dollar mark!" Janet did a happy dance and I skipped over to join her.

"Tax free?" I asked.

"Tax free!"

"Net or gross?"

"Net! After paying for the orphanage and the chapel twice and all the renovations..."

"...and the gravy kitchen and Precious Heart's costumes?" I held hands with Janet and did my best happy dance with absolutely no worries about falling down.

"Oh yeah..."

"Tax free." I loved tax free. "This is really working!"

"It's working so well, I'm tempted to propose to Buff," Janet said.

I stopped short in shock. "Really?"

Smiling from ear to ear Janet nodded.

"So you've told him about Biff?"

Suddenly solemn, Janet said, "Well, no. I thought we would save that for after the marriage. You know, so we will have something to talk about."

I gave Janet the look my mom always gave me when I said something stupid.

She held up a hand to ward me off. "Now, don't start. Just be proud of me for finally giving in. And be proud of us..." She began to chant again, "...we just made a million dollars, tax free. How awesome are we!"

Okay, fine. I was too happy to lecture. I sang back. "We made a million...in less than a year...we are woman, hear us roar!"

And then the idea hit! The perfect idea. I stopped what I was doing and stared into Janet's eyes, something she seldom let me do these days, since, you know, the naked exorcism incident. "We should throw a party! A big one and invite all our friends...oh, oh...and the Shameless Rat Bastards! We should invite them and thank them for screwing with our sign. If it hadn't been for the sign, I doubt we would be here today. Because, you know, the sign was a sign! Like a sign from God!"

Janet nodded. "Oh wait! My birthday is next week. Buff is already throwing me a party with a Maserati. Let's party on Daddy B's dime. What would be better when I tell him he can shove his blackmail scam? You can bring Monkey Boy!"

Well, that sobered me up. I sat down on the edge of the couch, now more than a bit bummed. "No, I can't."

"Aw, hun, didn't it work out for you two?"

"There never was a two. As soon as he was exorcised, he remembered his goal of boogie boarding to China and took off for the coast. I'm just as alone now as ever."

Bummer, huh? Only I didn't feel particularly bummed out. True he had amazing, record-breaking abs and hair that was thick and wavy and felt like heaven, and then there were those eyes. Those perfectly deep wells of childhood anticipation. No, what? Yeah, that was it. That was exactly what kept me from falling head over heels for the guy. With all his good looks and kind spirit, at heart, he was still a big ol' kid. He would forever be drawn to Jell-O pits and drinking too much and fun. While fun was good, I needed more than just fun. I needed devotion, maturity and ambition.

I shook it off. "I'll rent a date somewhere. One I can send home at the end of the night with no regrets."

"Ew, you mean one of those sleazy escort services?" Janet looked like she might puke.

"What? You'd rather I take Andrew and his missing tail scars?"

"Well, you have a point there, but we still have to invite him. He does work here now."

"Of course we do, just not as my escort," I said.

"Deal. Okay, I'll go revise my birthday party guest list. You hire an escort and talk Buff into exchanging the red Maserati for a blue one. Oh, and he should be prepared to hand over the sales receipt and title. I intend to take it back. Spending that kind of money on a car is ridiculous when I could use it to buy a tiara for the wedding!

"Is it wrong to have a white wedding at my age?"

"I don't think it is your age that may stand in the way of a white wedding," I said thinking of Biff and wondering if there was a way to find him in time for the party. If anyone could, I had faith Jake was the man for the job, now that his nose cast had come off.

"Yeah, maybe you're right. I'll just wear a silver sequined number. Silver, white. Same thing really." Janet giggled and clapped her hands. "I'm getting married. I'm rich, and I'm getting married to my childhood sweetheart. Okay, I'm off!"

Janet left, and I flipped on my computer, determined to carefully pick out my date for this event. I wanted someone who was mature but youthful. Conservative but a little bit crazy. I wanted someone light on his feet and attentive, who could hold an intelligent conversation on any topic but knew when to shut up. He had to be attentive—oh, I already said that—and handsome. Maybe a Gene Kelly type. Yeah. I always liked older men who had a sense of elegance about them.

I found a local escort service on the Internet. BestMan.net where men were men who knew how to treat women like queens. Nice, I could pay by the hour, day or week with a credit card or money order. No cash accepted but who accepted cash anymore? This was like shopping for a holiday dress. I browsed a gallery of men. Each profile featured a cameo and a full-length shot, and if I clicked on the banana peel in the corner, I got to see the unwrapped version of the man. The profile included measurements from the really personal kind—the kind I really didn't want to know until at least the third date—to shoe size, inseam, waist and shirt size. I also read about their preferences, hobbies and interests.

So many choices. I finally narrowed my search down to age range, height and availability, then education, dance proficiency and pure physical appeal. My choices became a lot more limited then. Apparently the call for older men from women my age was limited or the male escort business had a lucrative retirement package. The closest I found to a Gene Kelly lookalike was two inches shorter than I am and felt the perfect night out on the town was a night in. His favorite color was black, which I always considered as the absence of color, and he promised to rock my world all night long. Um, no. As the second clumsiest person on Earth—I'd decided long ago that Monkey Boy deserved first place—I'd spent way too much of my time flat on my back waiting for the end of the world. I settled on a towheaded thirty-something who preferred a night out with friends dancing and, ya know, hanging out. He had a master's in lit and owned, ya know, his own car. I checked out the money back guarantee and made my purchase.

At least he could dance.

Francine Zane

Chapter 31: It's My Party

The towheaded man showed up at my doorstep promptly at eight.

"Hi. My name is Kip. I'll be your escort tonight." He flashed me a million-dollar smile, which sort of made up for the name and the fact he was a paid escort. Not really, but it wasn't like anyone had forced me to do it.

I held out my hand and was surprised when he lifted it to his lips and placed a light kiss on the palm.

"Ah, thanks?" I said for lack of a better answer. No one had ever kissed my hand before. "My name is Lolla. Shall we go? I have a car waiting."

The car Buff had insisted on sending was spacious, but I still felt closed in with this stranger. We had twenty minutes to kill during the ride. It might have been the longest ride of my life.

"So, have you been in the business

long...you know...the...umm..." I wasn't sure how much I wanted to say with the driver listening in.

"The entertainment business?" Kip asked with a grin. "About five years. A buddy of mine said it might be a good fit for my personality."

"Do you enjoy it?"

"Sure! Free booze. Lots of new people." He leaned closer to me. "Beautiful women."

I was glad the interior of the car was dark. I wasn't accustomed to compliments either.

"Is that how you would like introduced tonight? As an entertainer?"

Kip leaned in closer, his lips almost touching my ear. "That is up to you. I am all yours for the evening. I'll be anyone you want me to be."

Before I recovered from the panic attack that he might actually touch me, he was back on his side of the backseat straightening his tie and looking out the side window.

"It's going to be a beautiful night," Kip said.

"Uh, huh," I said, my entire body shaking so bad I was for sure he could hear my teeth clattering against one another. I don't think I said another word the rest of the trip. I was too busy trying to relax enough to stop shaking.

I'm not sure why I was so shaken up. I was the customer here, and I wasn't even alone with him. The driver was right there just a yelp away. I had total control over what happened or didn't happen. Maybe that was it. Maybe I doubted that I could trust myself.

We arrived at the hotel where Biff had gone all out to set up a colossal party. The Maserati was parked in the lobby with a huge bow. Kip and I showed our invitations at the door and walked into a crowd of people. I spotted Andrew Ren head banging with a young blonde lady. Jake and Mrs. Hightower were waltzing near the bar. The two feminist we spoke to from the sign rally were there talking with Precious Heart. Mother Superior stood in a corner with her ruler at the ready. One sequined foot tapped to the music. The man at her side I deduced must have been her husband from the familiar arm he had wrapped around her waist. I made a note to introduce myself.

I recognized several members of the

congregation gathered around Henrietta and Henry. Buff had flown them in for the event. I didn't see Biff or Daddy B. And there was the guest of honor. Janet wore a demure black dress belted with rhinestones that glinted as the ballroom lights flashed over it. Buff played the dashing fiancé at her side. She spotted me and waved me over, making sure I caught sight of the giant rock on her right hand. She looked so happy.

I waved back and pointed Kip in the right direction. He took my hand and helped me weave the through the tightly packed throng. Halfway there, I spotted the tables we set aside for the Shameless Rat Bastards. They looked like the only people not having fun. Call me petty, but I had to make a detour and rub it in.

"Hi! Is everyone having a good time?" I asked the table of six men and two women, all of them looking as if they would rather be somewhere else.

The man I recognized as Dick Martin, the manager of the SRB located closest to Shyster and Shyster, answered. "Nice party, Lolla. Thanks for inviting us."

"Well, we couldn't have done it without you, Dick. If it hadn't been for you, Dick, and your sign sabotaging cohorts, we never would have had such a good season." I smiled my warmest, most welcoming smile.

Dick shook his head. "Honest, Lolla. I don't know what you are talking about."

"Oh, come off it. You sent people out to ruin our advertising campaign. You know it, and so do I."

"Believe what you want, Lolla." Dick picked up his empty drink and walked away.

"That's just what SRB is known for the most. Lying and walking away from problems," I said to the people remaining at the table.

I turned to go and noticed Kip giving me a questioning look. "Never mind," I said. "It's a long story."

We were almost to Janet when I saw something I never expected to see in an upscale hotel. With a Tarzan call, the long-missing son of Janet and Buff made a jaw-dropping entry from the second story balcony. Standing on the edge of the railing, he leaped out into the air and grabbed hold of a chandelier. Someone screamed and pointed, then everyone looked up.

"Hey, what does a boy have to do..." Biff

swung his body until the chandelier was rocking side to side. I prayed it would hold his weight. Then he swung from the chandelier to the disco ball and hugged it with his arms and legs, finally letting go with his arms to hang upside down. "...to get an invite to his own parents' engagement party?"

He swung over to grab the next chandelier and then made light work of pulling himself up to a standing position on it. "Yeah, Janet, Buff. I know what bad teenagers you were. Made a baby and gave it up, only Daddy B didn't like that plan. He brought me back in the family and still you couldn't tell me you was my 'rents."

I grabbed hold of Kip's arm and held it like a security blanket. Never in my wildest dreams would I have thought Biff would show up and like this!

"Boy, get your butt down here!" Daddy B stood at the edge of the stage where Janet and Biff had been holding court.

"Why? So you can hold something else over my head? You gonna spank me or just tell me how worthless my mother is again?"

Biff hung out over the crowd with one arm wrapped around the chandelier core and the other waving at us. "Tell them, Daddy B. Tell them how many years you held it over my head that you knew who my parents were before you ever told me. Tell them how you waited until your wife died—the only mother I ever really knew—to tell me the truth because she was the only one standing between me and your hatred."

"Get down, boy, and we'll talk," Daddy B waved Biff to come down, his expression a cross between angry and worried.

"You'd like that wouldn't you? Me to come straight down..." Biff wavered then caught his balance before he did a swan dive.

I stopped breathing as Kip's arms closed around me and crushed me against his chest. Around me, people screamed. It took me a couple of heartbeats to realize Biff was not falling to his death. I looked up from the safety of Kips embrace in time to see Biff travel along a zip line that was barely discernible in the soft lighting. He landed on his feet next to his mother and father, and pointed at Daddy B.

"This old man is evil. He's done everything possible to keep you two apart, and I'm here to say..." He took Janet by the arms and looked into her eyes. "...to say welcome to the family, Mom." He folded Janet into his arms and kissed her on top of her head. Then he turned to his dad, and they stared at one another for a long time.

"You're my boy?" Buff said.

"Yeah."

"I didn't know," Buff said. "Not until a few days ago. I'm sorry." His face screwed up in pain. "I didn't know."

And he fell into the nest of Biff and Janet's arms crying, but they weren't the only ones. I was crying. I heard others around me sniffling and saw both men and women wiping their eyes. The moment was truly unforgettable. Kip rubbed my back and handed me a handkerchief. So far, he was worth every penny I had paid for him.

Chapter 32: Cowabunga, Baby!

"Cowabunga, baby!" came a cry from the balcony and down came Andrew along the zip line, his long legs pulled up as he dropped close to people's heads. Unlike Biff and his perfect landing, Andrew flew past Janet and did a belly flop into the birthday cake. Pink frosting and checkerboard cake splattered everyone like a sugary sweet Gallagher finale. Only some dumbass forgot to provide the front rows with plastic sheeting.

I headed up to the remains of the once lovely six-foot tiered cake and my employee. How could the boy be so insensitive to what was going on here? I was ready to take him by the ear and escort him out of here.

"Boy, just what do you think you're doing?" I asked Andrew as he shook like a dog and littered me with another lay of frosted cake. The odor was so sweet that I thought I might never eat cake again.

"Oh, hi, Lolla! I didn't see you come in." He slipped and slid his way to his feet, then skated to my side and put an arm around my shoulders.

I rolled my eyes and kissed my dress goodbye. I might have been more upset if he hadn't already sprayed me with foodstuffs.

Andrew Ren slurred his words in an exaggerated whisper. "Did you know I'm a spy?" He poked a finger at my chest with each word. "A dirty, nasty spy who has spent the last year spying on his best friends because he is a spy. A dirty, nasty, sign-tampering spy." With a wail, he buried his face into my neck and cried.

"Get off me!" I pushed the drunk intern back into his bakery bed. "What do you mean by spy?"

Andrew lay where he fell and created a cake and tear paste that I hoped would glue him to the floor until he sobered up. "I don't deserve to be here. I don't deserve friends like you and Guide Precious." He cradled his head in his hands and continued to lament. "Precious! She's gonna kick my ass when she finds out what I did."

"Boy, talk!" I snapped with my best mean boss voice.

"Yeah, talk," Janet said as she walked up beside me, perfectly manicured hands on her hips.

"Daddy B. He wanted me to keep an eye on you. He promised to pay off my student loans, and I got a buttload of student loans. So, I been keeping an eye on you." He pointed to his eye and then to Janet and me. "I'm still waiting to get paid." He'd stopped crying but now he was busy trying to figure out how to unwind his legs and stand. All he managed to do was slip down into the cake again with a new spray of debris, but I hardly noticed.

I was watching Janet confront her father-in-law-to-be.

"You are behind all of this...this mess? Why? What did I ever do to you?" Janet's voice was heavy with emotion.

"This isn't the place for this discussion," Daddy B said.

"Really? After all the family laundry already aired here, thanks to you, you are now concerned about protecting your privacy? Isn't that kind of like closing the gate after the cows got out? So answer me. What have I ever done to you to deserve all this." Janet waved at the ruins of her once lovely party where now all eyes were on her but for all the wrong reasons.

The old man looked Janet up and down. Even sprinkled with cake guts, he maintained his dignity. "What makes you think anything I do is about you? You are nothing."

"I am your future daughter-in-law."

"Over my dead body!" Daddy B said.

Buff stepped between his ladylove and father. "I am marrying her, Daddy. I told you that when I was sixteen, and I've told you that every year since."

"Like hell you will!"

The men were standing inches apart. Father and son, so much alike and yet on opposite sides of the issue. Beyond my own fury at Daddy B for his control issues, I felt for the men. As crazy as my family was, they never stood in my way, not when I really set my mind to do something. They certainly didn't try to sabotage me.

"Answer Janet's question, Dad," Buff said. "Why have you done all of this?"

Daddy B looked like a roomful of trained interrogators would never pull the truth out of him, and then he melted. It was as if all the eyes in the room trained on him drained him of his resolve.

"Buff, it's not Janet," Daddy B's voice was soft but carried in the silence of the room as the crowd watched the exchanged. "It's that father of hers. Shyster Mike and I used to be partners, just like these two women." He pointed to Janet and me. "That was before he got greedy and started his shady dealings, and that was before I got into physical fitness. Mike was dating Netty, Buff's mother, so she was always around. I got to know her, and we became friends. Shyster Mike didn't take kindly to Netty having a male friend, and it caused some friction between the two of them. The more friction Netty faced, the more she leaned on me for support.

"Next thing I know, Shyster Mike was in jail, and Netty was on my doorstep asking me to hide her. Netty looked like she'd been hit by a truck. I assumed Mike had beaten her up and took her in. Mike and I were over. We sold the business and went our own ways. It wasn't until years later that Netty told me Shyster Mike wasn't the one who hit her. He'd tried to protect her and ended up in jail for attacking her abuser. He never told me that, probably because I never gave him a chance. When Netty finally confessed, she said she never told me because she didn't want Mike and me to be friends. If we were friends, I'd find out her own father beat her for not breaking up with Mike and taking up with me. You see, her father felt I had more potential than Mike."

"Old man, you are stalling. What does this have to do with me?" Janet said.

"Netty was pregnant when she came to me. With Mike's child. Buff is that child."

Whoa! I wasn't expecting that one. I could have believed Shyster Mike screwed Daddy B over. Shyster Mike screwed over a lot of people but never had I heard one whisper about a violent disposition.

Janet looked as shocked as I did. Shocked and ashamed. Who wants to be told the man you love is your half-brother, especially in such a public manner.

I went to my friend and put an arm around her shoulder. Buff had taken a step back, my guess, at the concept of who she represented and not her as a woman. You don't chase a woman for that many years just to let go so easily. We were all in shock, but I couldn't imagine being in Buff and Janet's positions, or Biff for that matter. He didn't look so shocked. Maybe Daddy B had already told him. Maybe after so many years of torture at Daddy B's hands, he was numb to anything else the man had to say.

"He lies!" A man's voice came from the rear of the ballroom.

I whipped around and saw the crowd parting for an older man who looked vaguely familiar. It took me a minute to place him.

"Shyster Mike," I whispered.

"Daddy B lies, and he knows it," Mike reiterated as he came to stand near the core group.

"How did you get here? You're supposed to be in jail," Daddy B said.

"Welcome to the real world, Daddy B, where the prison system is so overloaded that even a man like me can get early parole," Shyster Mike said. "Now back to that story. Do you want to rethink it just a bit?"

Daddy B backed up slowly, never taking his eyes from Mike. He backed up until he had nowhere else to back. Mike never moved. None of us moved, and yet I could feel the animosity in the air. The atmosphere felt like kindling just waiting for a match strike.

Daddy B cringed, "Don't hurt me."

"I'm not going to hurt you," Shyster Mike said. "But you are going to tell the truth, or I'll tell the authorities what I know about your physical fitness kingdom. How do you think they would react to mon—"

Daddy B jumped to attention. "Okay. Stop. Yeah, maybe I got some of the facts a little lopsided. Netty was my girlfriend. But she was pregnant when she moved in with me. She didn't move in until after she told me she was pregnant. I kind of, well, I didn't receive the news well. She'd just gotten back from a business trip with Mike. When I confronted Mike, we got into a fight, and she tried to break it up. I accidentally elbowed her in the eye, and she fell."

"Tell them all of it Bernard..." Shyster Mike said.

Bernard? Daddy B's real name is Bernard? No wonder he kept that a secret. No matter how good his body may have looked in his prime, the name Bernard would do nothing to improve his sex appeal.

Daddy B visibly gulped and continued, refusing to meet the gaze of anyone. "She lost the baby. We didn't conceive Buff for another year."

"Now tell Janet why you are taking this out on her," Mike demanded.

"Mike, you can't put this all on me. You're responsible, too."

Mike drew back his fist and leaned toward Daddy B.

Daddy B shielded himself. "Okay, okay! I targeted Janet because...I didn't just target Janet. Ever since Mike and I had a falling out, I've been taking over as many of Mike's businesses as I can. I hate the man. I hate that he made me look bad in front of my woman. I hate his success, and I hate you, Janet. I hate that you exist. I hate that you are the one thing Mike has that I can't take away from him. And worst of all, I know my son loves you more than me. You marry Buff, and I'll lose all the family I have left. Netty's gone..." Daddy B melted with tears rolling down his ruddy cheeks. "Biff hates me. Now Buff will hate me, too."

I couldn't blame anyone for hating him. I didn't though. I felt sorry for him, but he had played so many games with so many people. Andrew had betrayed people he loved because of Daddy B. Shyster and Shyster was sabotaged by Andrew. True, Andrew sucked at sabotage, and we had succeeded. Janet and Buff had been kept apart for years. And then there was Biff, who had been punished over and over because he personified the very fears Daddy B had fought for ages.

Shyster Mike must have been satisfied with what he heard. He turned away from the pathetic Daddy B and back to his family. Janet, Buff and Biff, the grandson he had yet to meet. I backed off. This was family time.

"Kip?" I said.

"Yeah?" Kip said.

"Take me home."

What had started out as a dream, ended as an exhausting confession. Tomorrow, Janet may need me as a friend, but for now she was covered, and all I wanted to do was take my shoes off, clean up and have a hot chocolate. I might even call my mother. She looked like pretty good family compared to what I had seen tonight.

Epilogue

Shyster Mike reopened Shyster and Shyster with the help of his grandson Biff. They asked Andrew to come back as an intern, but Andrew decided to become a disciple of Precious Heart and made a vow of poverty. Considering how much he owed in student loans, I'm not sure exactly how much he gave up.

At the party, Precious Heart met a lovely feminist hiking guide from Alaska. She took a sabbatical to spend some time with her new ladylove. In the meantime, Mother Superior led our Sunday services. Attendance went down by twenty percent, but we have faith that Precious can pull the numbers back up when she gets back.

Lizzy Deadbeat came around during the next filing tax season with another horde of children. We filed the return for her since she had the paperwork to prove she could claim them, then took the kids to the orphanage where Mother Superior cleaned them up and went to work on their education and religious training. With luck, at least one of the orphans will be prepared to take over for Precious in a couple of decades when and if she decides to retire.

Mrs. Hightower officially adopted Jake into her family shortly before her demise. She left him her entire estate. Jake invested heavily in the fashion industry and opened an upscale men's shoe shop. As add-on services, he added an old-timey shoeshine stand and lessons on how to get the most shine on your shoe. Next year, he launches his own line of shoeshine polishes.

Monkey Boy made it to China this time. He decided to stay when he met a swimsuit model who could bench press as much as he could. Next month his goes under the knife to have the sweaty towel scar removed from his all too perfect body.

Sar Rah, on the other hand, found out her drunk baby was actually a tumor. See there, Arnold Schwarzenegger. Sometimes it really is a tumor! She delivered the largest known tumor in history then partied her way into a guest spot on Jerry Springer where she smashed a chair over the head of a girlfriend who called her a money grubbing boy toy. Last month, she won the first national twerking competition in Fargo, North Dakota—the unofficial twerking capital of the world.

Henry and Henrietta went back to Florida after the party. Henrietta is now a regular on *Storage Wars*. With her earnings from the show, she purchased an abandoned factory and had it renovated into her new home. Now she has much more space in which to partake in hoarding.

Darla Fishbourne, aka Tasty Tushy, remained a loyal client and church member for many years. She did three more calendars and two movies that she publicized as *erotic pleasure isn't just for the young.* I never saw either of her movies. I pray I never do.

Pussy Feet became a well-known rapper. He remained a member of the church and had six pews installed in the back of the auditorium. Pussy Feet permanently reserved the pews for his crew.

We brought the radical feminists into the fold, and they now reside in the commune of the Church of Perpetual Profits. They continue to deliver vengeance against the wicked and provide temporary housing for abuse victims. During their off time, they have taken over the exorcism duties. Exorcism is our third most lucrative profit center.

Janet and Buff had a beautiful wedding. Buff moved in with Janet after disowning his father. They are expecting their second and third children. Yes, twins. Janet continues to be the powerhouse behind our success. I would be lost without her.

Daddy B lives all alone in his big house. He sold his physical fitness empire to an Asian conglomerate. His butt has fallen six inches since then. The only time anyone has seen him is when he walks to the mailbox.

Kip, my towheaded escort, became my dance instructor. It turns out he is the great, great grandson of some vaudeville actor turned Hollywood movie star who shall remain nameless. Let's just say grandpa liked singing in the rain. So maybe I made the right escort choice to begin with. Next month we enter our first dance competition. If we win, Kip plans to retire from the escort business and use our winnings to open a dance studio.

My Me account has grown exponentially

with the size of our congregation. Next year, we hope to expand the Church of Perpetual Profits to five new locations nationwide. If all goes according to our business plan, the Me account will hit the magic number, and I will retire from the fascinating world of tax preparation sans religious leader. Oh, I won't sell out. That would be just crazy, but I will become a silent partner. Janet doesn't really need me anyway. I've always left all the heavy lifting to her. I'm more of an idea kind of girl.

When the Me account hits the magic number, I'm headed to Hollywood. I've got a movie in me somewhere, and the account will allow me to be the creative mastermind behind the very first all-female cross-dressing musical. Think *Hair* meets *Annie* meets *Yentl* meets *Beach Blanket Bingo.* Yeah! With my mind for business and the script I bought off of eBay, I anticipate a big, big hit. Hey, Kip can be our choreographer, and I can likely talk Jake into buying into the project. Now if only I can find an unknown actress who has the charisma of Precious, the style of Mother Superior, the work ethic of Janet, the buns of Buff and my smile...

Francine Zane

The End

About the Author

Francine Zane is a humor writer who lives and breathes in the great Midwest. She spends her days catering to the whims of the general public and her evenings cowering in a corner praying her cats do not eat her while she sleeps.

Francine spent her youth channeling the ever-delightful personality of a beached whale. Now she shares her observations with whoever is too slow or stupid to run away.

Website: www.francinezane.com
FB: FrancineZane
Twitter: @FrancineZane
Google+: Francine Zane
Instagram: @FrancineZane